ON THE FENCE

Also by Kasie West

Pivot Point
Split Second

The Distance Between Us

ON THE FENCE

KASIE WEST

HARPER TEEN

An Imprint of HarperCollinsPublishers

*To Michelle Wolfson,
who in the process of helping me fulfill my dreams
has become a true friend*

HarperTeen is an imprint of HarperCollins Publishers.

On the Fence
Copyright © 2014 by Kasie West
All rights reserved. Printed in the United States of America.
No part of this book may be used or reproduced in any manner whatsoever
without written permission except in the case of brief quotations
embodied in critical articles and reviews. For information address
HarperCollins Children's Books, a division of HarperCollins
Publishers, 195 Broadway, New York, NY 10007.
www.harpercollinschildrens.com

Library of Congress Cataloging-in-Publication Data
West, Kasie.
On the fence / Kasie West. — First edition.
   pages cm
Summary: "Sixteen-year-old Charlie has always been a tomboy,
but when she accidentally becomes a makeup model, her newfound
femininity draws her into an unknown social world, complete with guy
troubles she's never had before"— Provided by publisher.
   ISBN 978-0-06-223567-1 (pbk. bdg.)
   [1. Self-actualization (Psychology)—Fiction. 2. Sex role—Fiction.
3. Brothers and sisters—Fiction. 4. Single-parent families—Fiction.
5. Dating (Social customs)—Fiction. 6. Family life—California—Fiction.
7. California—Fiction.] I. Title.
   PZ7.W51837On 2014   2013021358
   [Fic]—dc23   CIP
                                                              AC

Typography by Torborg Davern
18 19 20   PC/LSCH   20 19 18 17 16
❖
First Edition

CHAPTER 1

• • • • • • •

The engine whined against my attempt to go faster. The yellow lines of the road went by on my left in a blur. The ocean on my right didn't seem affected at all. It created the illusion that I wasn't going fast enough. The gentle curves on this road begged to be taken at high speeds. I pushed down another inch on the gas pedal and the car lurched forward. My heart picked up speed and I couldn't keep the smile from my face. Wind whipped through the cabin, sending my hair flying and drying the sweat on my forehead from my last practice of the school year.

Red and blue lights flashed in the rearview mirror. I pointlessly lifted my foot off the gas pedal, as if that would help. I looked for a place to pull off the road, already coming up with my story. By the time the cop reached my window, pad in hand, I'd thought of two great possibilities.

When I saw his face, all my excuses were gone. I sighed and rolled down the window.

"Charlotte Reynolds, we meet again," he said.

"Hi, officer."

"What is this, the third time?"

"Is it?" Crap. What were the odds the same cop had to pull me over three times? "My dad says hi."

He laughed. "Your dad is a good cop, but his name isn't going to get you out of it this time. Not when you were going fifteen miles over the speed limit."

"Really? It couldn't have been fifteen."

"It was. I need your license."

"Can I look at your radar, make sure you read it right?"

He raised his eyebrows at me and I grudgingly handed over my license. My dad was going to kill me.

I walked in the front door and threw my bag under the entryway table, still angry about the stupid ticket. "Where is everyone?" I yelled out. I followed the sounds of laughter into the kitchen. A blender sat in the middle of the island, surrounded by a bottle of Tabasco sauce, ketchup, and eggshells. Gage looked up and caught my eye.

"Charlie! Just in time."

I could smell from the doorway whatever awful smoothie they had just created—it smelled like rotten tomatoes. "Oh no."

"Oh yes." Nathan snaked his arm around my shoulder and pulled me up to the counter. "Grab another glass."

A glass was added to the others on the counter. "On three we down it," Gage said, pouring some of the soupy concoction from the blender into five glasses.

"Why are we doing this?" I asked, looking at the four guys around the kitchen island. Three of them were my brothers—Jerom, Nathan, and Gage—and the other might as well have been—Braden. He'd been our neighbor for twelve of the sixteen years of my life and was always around.

"One, to prove we can. Two, to toughen our stomachs for the pounding they're going to get in football tomorrow."

"So, in other words, just to be idiots."

"That too," Gage said, holding up his glass. "Ready?"

"Losers have to wear it," Braden said.

"Yeah, yeah, come on already. I want to run before dark." I took a closer whiff. I shouldn't have. It smelled worse than Gage's closet.

"She's not going to do it. Charlie's chickening out," Nathan said, pointing at me.

"No, you're stalling." He was right. I wasn't going to drink it. But neither were they. That was the whole game here. We had done this before. Well, not this particular one, but various versions over the years. *On the count of three, everyone jump in the pool. On the count of three, everyone yell, "I'm a loser," in the middle of the mall. On the count of three, everyone lick the person to your right.* It was a game of bluff. If one person did it, the rest had to do something stupid as a punishment. If nobody did it, everyone was safe.

The only person I was wary of in that moment was Braden. My brothers were so easy to read. Tonight, I knew they weren't going to drink it the minute I'd walked into the kitchen—it was written all over their faces, twisted in disgust. But Braden, even after all these years, was still the wild card. I eyed him and he smiled at me.

Scared? he mouthed.

I shook my head and studied his eyes. They were hazel, sometimes more green and sometimes more brown. They seemed more green at that moment, and I tried to figure out what that meant about his intention. Was he going to drink it?

"Okay, close your eyes," Jerom said. "Glasses ready."

I closed my eyes. I did not want to wear this and have to take two showers tonight—before and after the run.

"One . . ."

Braden cleared his throat next to me. That was a bluff move, wasn't it? So that meant he wasn't going to drink it.

"Two . . ."

He bumped his elbow into mine. Crap, he was trying to trick me. So that meant he *was* going to drink it.

"Three."

Better to drink it than to wear it. I downed the glass in three big gulps, gagging only slightly.

"Charlie!" Nathan whined. "Seriously?"

They all held a full glass in front of them. "Ha! Wear it. All of you." I looked at Braden, who had a smug look on his face even though technically he'd lost. I had to learn his tell so in the future I could avoid the horrid taste that coated my tongue. My stomach wasn't very happy either. "Mmm, tastes like V8."

"Ew, Charlie, never date a guy who likes V8," Gage said.

I rolled my eyes. Ever since I turned sixteen—the age my father's dating ban officially lifted—my brothers constantly spouted off qualities they thought made a guy undateable. I was convinced that if I compiled all the things they had rattled off in the last six months, there would be no one in the world left for me to date. "Why not?" I asked.

"Because you can't trust a guy who drinks his vegetables. Plus tomato-juice breath is raunchy."

My entire mouth slowly heated up from the Tabasco sauce. Then I got a punch of pepper that made me gag. "Ugh. What did you guys put in that?" I turned around and gave my tongue a high-pressure wash under the kitchen tap. "There is no pouring going on," I said, spitting water everywhere. I listened as they dumped the horrible concoction on their heads to groans and complaints. Not worth the taste in my mouth. I gurgled and spit out one more mouthful of water. "Okay, that was fun. Football tomorrow. You are all going down." I shoved Braden on my way out of the kitchen and he laughed, obviously knowing he was the only reason I ended up downing the drink.

"Wait," Jerom called. "I want to run with you."

"I'm not waiting for you to shower." I crouched down and tightened my laces.

He slicked his hair back, the Tabasco sauce tingeing his black hair red. "Who said anything about showering? Let me grab my shoes."

The smell lingering around Jerom as we ran made me sick to my stomach. Probably because the smell reminded me of what sat in my stomach. It didn't help that it was a muggy summer night. Heat combined with moisture was not my favorite running condition.

I distracted myself by trying to identify the trees in the park. I knew the big ones were eucalyptus. They grew all up and down the coast. They must've liked the salty air. Even where we lived, ten miles from the ocean, they thrived.

"Eight weeks of summer," Jerom said, interrupting my failed attempt to name any more trees. "Then we'll be shackled by the oppressive chains again."

"Don't remind me. At least you have some freedom."

"You think college equals freedom?"

"Uh . . . yes!"

He laughed. "Okay, yeah, it kind of does. But I still have classes and soccer, so it's not as free as it could be."

"Have you warned Nathan? I think he's been looking forward to some freedom."

"Yeah, right. If there weren't rules to stay within the strict confines of, Nathan wouldn't know what to do with himself."

"True."

He glanced over at me, slightly out of breath. It was good to know I could still outrun my big brother. I wasn't even winded. "What about you?" he asked. "Any preconceived notions about being an upperclassman I need to crush?"

"Oh, please, I've been an upperclassman for two years

already, considering I've hung out with Nathan, Gage, and Braden my whole high school career."

"True. Maybe they did you a disservice with that. Maybe they should've let you suffer in the trenches for a while before calling you up."

"Maybe I should race you up the hill." I pointed ahead of us. The hill marked the beginning of mile three. My stomach gurgled, not agreeing with my suggestion, but as soon as Jerom said "You're on," I couldn't back down.

As we powered up the hill, I noticed for the first time that it wasn't just muggy; dark clouds hung overhead. Rain clouds. He led for the first fifty yards or so, but it was a big hill. I saved my speed for when he lost his energy, and I raced past him. At the top, I bent over, now winded, and tried to catch my breath.

"Being a forward has spoiled you," I said. "I hear mid-fielders all over the world collectively laughing at you."

"Whatever."

"It looks like it's going to rain," I said, glancing at the sky again. "We better still be able to play tomorrow."

"Oh, we'll play. It just might turn into mud football." He looked at his sleeve and then flicked a chunk of red goo off it.

The visual made my stomach flip, and acid crept up the back of my throat. "Hold on a minute." I walked to the side of the road and proceeded to puke in some bushes. The smell made me want to repeat the action, but I quickly walked away.

"Gross," Jerom said.

I wiped my mouth with the back of my hand. "Yeah, those raw eggs mixed with Tabasco don't sit very well. But I feel much better now." And I did. "Let's go." I ran again, heading toward the path that led around the park and then back down into our neighborhood.

"Do you ever think you push yourself too hard?" Jerom asked, once he was beside me.

"This, coming from Mr. I Go to UNLV on a Soccer Scholarship?" I remembered when he was first awarded that scholarship. Even though Nevada was his dream school, I had secretly hoped for a closer college. It was hard to let go of any of my brothers. I wanted to keep them close. Safe. I was happy when he decided to come home during the summers. "No, I don't think I push myself too hard. You gotta do your best to be the best, right?"

"I guess."

"You guess? You're the one who always says that. The quote was taped to your bedroom door for years. Don't give me this 'I guess.' Besides"—I pointed back toward the bushes—"that had nothing to do with pushing myself, and you know it. I'm not even tired. That had to do with a drink I shouldn't have partaken of, the remnants of which you still have all over your shirt."

"True." We jogged a few more yards. "Why did you?"

"Why did I what?"

"Why did you drink it? You knew we weren't going to."

But I didn't know Braden wouldn't. "Like that time I knew you weren't going to kiss a random stranger? You did. All of you did, even Nathan, and I was stuck telling the next four people I saw that I thought I was in love with my dog and asking if they knew where I could find help for it."

He laughed so hard he had to stop running for a minute. "The punishment was funny, but the challenge was easy. That's why we all did it. What was your deal? You didn't like the random stranger we picked for you to kiss?"

"Something like that." Actually, the random stranger was pretty cute. My issue was that I didn't think he'd welcome my advances. My brothers were cool. Attractive. Most girls even described them as hot, with their tall, athletic builds and stormy gray eyes. I'm sure the girls they'd kissed that day still talked about it.

I was . . . a tomboy. That day at the mall, the kiss-a-random-stranger day, I was wearing warm-ups from basketball practice, my hair was greasy and pulled up into a ponytail, and my lips were chapped. I wasn't kissing some random cute guy who probably would've gagged. "He wouldn't have been able to handle my awesomeness," I said out loud when I could tell Jerom was waiting for a better answer.

"Not many can put up with your awesomeness."

Ever since his laughing fit, we had slowed to a walk, and now I picked up the pace. "I think that was meant as an insult, but I will take it as you agreeing with me. Now let's move. No more slacking."

"Yes, coach."

When we got home I felt sticky and rubber-legged, but my lungs were open and adrenaline coursed through my body. It was one of the reasons I ran—this high I felt.

That night after collapsing into bed, I fell asleep immediately and slept like the dead—not a single dream.

And that was the other reason I ran.

CHAPTER 2

• • • • • • •

Apparently, it rained all night—not that I heard it—leaving the park a soggy mess. But, like Jerom said, perfect for mud football. My team huddled and Jerom looked at me. "Get open, it's coming to you. And, Charlie, it might help if you turn out instead of in this time."

"You worry about your technique, I'll worry about mine," I said.

"Just a suggestion."

"I know how to play."

"Yeah, Jerom. Charlie knows how to play," Gage teased, bumping his shoulder into mine. "Don't tell her what to do."

"Gage." Out of all my brothers, he was the closest to me, the only one I'd let get away with saying that. Mostly because he flashed me that cheesy smile of his and I couldn't stay mad at him.

"Good, then let's do this." Jerom clapped his hands and we lined up. The score was tied at seven with five minutes left. My socks were soggy with mud and my hands slipped off my knees as I crouched down, but I was going to catch this ball. I took off after the snap and Jerom threw a perfect pass. I caught it and ran. Someone grabbed hold of the back of my shirt and I shook him free, nearly sliding across the slick grass.

When there were no defenders between me and the orange cones, I started calling out my own plays. "She hurdles a puddle and spins into the end zone. Touch-down!" I turned around and held the ball in the air like a trophy. "Oh yeah! We are the best!"

"Stop gloating," Braden mumbled, picking himself up off the ground. "It's annoying."

"Sore loser," I coughed under my breath. He was just like my brothers—he hated to lose.

He put me in a headlock and rubbed his knuckles across my scalp.

A whiff of wet grass, sweat, and dirt filled my nose. "Ugh. You smell. Get off me."

"That's the stench of victory."

"More like the stink of failure."

He let me go right above a mud puddle, making sure to throw me off balance. I landed on my hands, splattering mud all over my face.

"You are dead." I jumped on him from behind, digging my knee in his lower back.

He let out a yell-laugh. When I slid off, I went to the sidelines, found his sweatshirt, then wiped my face clean with it. I headed back toward the field, where some guys were huddled together, including two of my brothers—Nathan and Jerom. "What are we all standing around for? Let's finish this thing."

Jerom and Nathan both shot me a warning look of silence. It wasn't until I got closer that I realized one of the guys, Dave, was on the phone.

"No girlfriend emergencies right now. We're in the middle of the game," I said, and Dave looked up but his eyes didn't focus on me.

"Charlie, shush," Nathan said. "Something's going on."

Several more guys crowded in. "What's up?" Braden asked from right behind me.

I shrugged. "I don't know, I've been shushed." Over Braden's shoulder I could see Gage by the starting line tossing the ball in the air over and over. He caught my eye and put his arms out in the "What's taking so long?" gesture. I just shook my head.

Finally, Dave hung up the phone and said, "I have to go. It's my grandma."

"Did you explain to your grandma that we're in the middle of a game?" I asked.

"She died."

"Oh."

A round of groans and apologies went around the group. Dave looked like he was in shock, his eyes glassed over.

"How old was she?" I asked.

He absently ran his hand along his shoulder. "Seventy-something. I'm not sure."

"What happened?"

"She's had cancer for about a year. We knew this was coming. We just weren't sure when."

"That sucks." I rubbed my hands together and looked around. Everyone just stood there, not sure what to say. "Should we finish the game, then?"

Braden elbowed me in the side.

"What? It will get his mind off it. And we only have five minutes left. We can't quit now."

"Charlie," Jerom said in his official big-brother scold, at the same time Nathan took one of my arms and Braden took the other, dragging me away from the group.

"What's the big de—" I couldn't finish my sentence because Braden clamped his hand over my mouth.

"We, of all people, should understand this," Nathan said under his breath. "Show a little empathy."

I bit down on Braden's finger and he let go. Then I yanked free of their hold. "What should I understand about some lady dying of a disease she'd been fighting?"

Braden reached out, probably trying to cover my mouth again. I stepped out of his reach.

"Shhh!" Nathan hissed, looking over his shoulder. "You should understand that—"

"Fine. Whatever. Tell Dave I'm sorry." With that, I turned and ran, taking the path around the park, then farther. Why should I understand what Dave was going through? Because someone in his life had died, like someone in my life had? Our situations were nothing alike. My mom had been thirty-one when she died. I hardly got to know her at all. I got a measly six years with her. Six years I didn't even remember.

The tightness in my chest made it hard to breathe, which made it hard to run. And that made me angry. Running was never hard for me. I forced myself to run until I could breathe normally again. It took a while.

By the time I got home, the sun was high in the sky and I was covered in sweat. Braden stood in my front yard. His wet-from-a-shower auburn hair looked black. He was a little taller than my brothers, which made him lankier, yet his broad shoulders made it obvious he was an athlete. "Hey, feel better?" he asked.

"Smell better?" I said with a smile.

"So that's a yes?"

"I'm fine. Apparently, I'm just a jerk, but we all knew that."

Braden cringed. He hated the word *jerk*. It's what we all called his dad—well, what Braden called him, and we all agreed. It was as if he felt that word belonged to his dad and was too big of an insult to assign to anyone else.

"So is Dave okay?"

"Jerom drove him home, so I'm sure he's fine."

"What's up with Jerom? Two years in college and suddenly he's all fatherly?"

"Your brother has always been a good listener."

He has? And why would Braden know that? I pointed to his driveway and the white work truck parked there. "Your dad got off early today?"

He waved his hand through the air, swatting away the question that apparently didn't merit a verbal response, then turned back to me. "What are you doing right now?"

"Showering." I reached my front door then turned around. "See ya."

He stopped me by saying, "We're going out for my mom's birthday tonight. I figured I better go to the mall and find her a present."

"Probably a good idea."

My hand was on the doorknob when he asked, "Any ideas for what to get her?"

"You're asking me?" I laughed. "Funny."

"I could use a girl's opinion."

"Then you better go find one."

"Well, opinion or not, you want to come?"

"To the mall?" I turned around. He had a look in his eye. Braden may have been a wild card, but I could still read him most of the time, and right now he felt sorry for me. Pity made me angry. "Look, Braden, I'm fine, okay?" And apparently if I needed to talk, Jerom's ear was available.

He held up his hands in surrender. "Fine." His eyes seemed to say, *Perhaps you do have a cold, cold heart, Charlie.* I couldn't have agreed more.

CHAPTER 3

• • • • • • •

Nathan was in charge of dinner that night and had just pulled some sort of pasta-and-meat dish out of the oven, timing it perfectly with my dad's arrival. *Kiss-up.* As my dad walked into the kitchen from the garage, he found where I sat at the table and narrowed his eyes at me. I wondered which one of my brothers had tattled and why my dad was so upset about it. For heaven's sake, what was everyone's problem? If I had started crying over Dave's grandma my life would've been a whole lot easier right then. Maybe I needed to practice some fake waterworks.

My dad was a nice guy and most of the time a pushover,

but when he was in his full police garb and had that look on his face, he terrified me. He hung his keys on a hook by the door, then unbuckled and hung his utility belt as well, the heavy flashlight banging the wall as he did. "Charlie . . . ," he said in a tired voice.

"I'm sorry." Then I made sure to give all my brothers a death glare. Gage played all big-eyed and innocent.

"You should be, but that's not going to be good enough this time."

"This time?" Had I been insensitive to the relatives of a different dead grandma before?

My dad approached the table and plopped a pink copy of my speeding ticket in front of me. Oh. This was worse than being insensitive. This was about breaking the law.

I tried to talk my way out of it. "I didn't know the speed limit and I didn't see him. He was hiding down a side street. Isn't that illegal, like entrapment or something? Nathan? Isn't that illegal?"

Nathan hid a smile and brought a pitcher of ice water to the table. Nathan was starting his first year of college next year. His ultimate goal—lawyerhood.

My dad leveled a hard stare at me. "Why didn't you tell me about it?"

"I'm sorry." I should've been honest. It was always worse when he found out about things from an outside source.

"This is the second ticket in as many months. And that's not counting the ones you got out of by using my name."

I ducked my head to hide the heat I could feel on my cheeks at having been caught. I didn't need my brothers making fun of me for blushing. My dad was right. I had been pulled over multiple times. I used his name every time.

"Do you know how embarrassing it is when my kids get speeding tickets? When I have to find out about those speeding tickets from a coworker?"

"I'm sorry."

"But worse than the embarrassment you caused me is the blow to my bank account." His finger came down hard on the pink slip, landing on a number written in his own handwriting that read *$264.00*. My eyes widened. "Yeah, that's a lot of money."

I nodded.

"You're paying for it."

"What?"

"You heard me. I don't think you learned your lesson last time because I paid for your ticket. So, you are paying not only for this ticket, but also the last one, *and* the extra hundred dollars a month you are going to cost me in insurance."

"But I don't have that kind of money."

"Then find a job."

"How? Basketball camp starts in about seven weeks, and then there's school and soccer after that."

"Dad," Gage piped in, using his winning smile in my defense this time. "Charlie's just a little girl. Don't make her work. She'll never survive."

Okay, so that wasn't exactly the defense I was looking for.

"Gage. Stay out of this," my dad said.

He saluted. "Yes, officer."

My dad turned his hard stare on Gage, but just like the rest of us, he couldn't stay mad at Gage either. So he turned back to me. "Figure it out, because it's my final decision." With that, he left the kitchen and went to his room to change. My brothers all stared at me and then, as if they'd counted to three, started laughing at exactly the same time.

"Yeah, it's so funny," I said. "As if you've never been pulled over before."

Nathan raised his hand. "Never." *Of course not.*

"Twice," Jerom said.

I looked at Gage. Of all my brothers, he and I were not only the closest but the most alike. "A few times," he said, "but I always got out of tickets. You gotta act a little more innocent, Charlie. You can't be belligerent with the cops. They don't like it."

"How do you know I was?"

They all laughed again. This round of laughter was cut off by the ringing of a cell phone, from where it sat being charged on the counter. Gage jumped up and slid across the island to answer it before it went to voice mail.

My dad came back, and the change in his clothes seemed to change his demeanor as well. He kissed the top of my head. Maybe this meant he was rethinking the whole job thing. "You should probably start looking first thing tomorrow," he said. Then he looked at Gage and snapped, "Off the phone."

I sank down farther in my chair and spooned myself some of Nathan's pasta creation. My dad said a prayer (being a cop for the last twenty years had put the fear of God in him). Then we all dug in. Dinner in our house was like a race. If you didn't eat fast, you missed out on seconds. I didn't feel much like seconds anyway.

I lay on my bed, feet up on the headboard, and threw a tennis ball against the wall over and over. There was a single knock on my door, and then someone I assumed was Gage let himself in. He was the only one who never waited for an answer. I tilted my head back and saw an upside-down version of Gage right before he took a flying leap and landed on my head.

I grunted my disapproval and he rolled off.

"So, a job, huh?"

"Don't remind me."

"I think this day should go down in history as the day Dad decreed one of his offspring must seek employment."

"Seriously. Whatever happened to 'School is your job' or 'Sports can pay for college so I consider that your job'?"

"Apparently, someone by the name of Speed Racer changed that." He paused and—just like Gage to always see the positive in something (which was one of the only ways we weren't alike)—said, "Finding a job is way better than getting grounded. If you were grounded, all the indoor air your body isn't used to breathing would dry out your pores and cause you to wither up and die."

Okay, maybe not *positive*, per se, but close to it.

He pushed his bangs off his forehead. "Well, for what it's worth, I offer you my job-hunting prowess."

"Which consists of?"

"Accompanying you and pointing to the stores you should pick up applications from, helping you write your name in little boxes. You know, invaluable stuff like that."

"What would I do without you?"

"It's too painful to even consider, but it might involve drying pores and withering."

CHAPTER 4

● ● ● ● ● ● ●

I came out of Urban Chic carrying an application and had to wait while Gage finished talking to a redhead and her short friend. I listened to the sound of the ocean, only three blocks away, and took a deep breath of coastal air. Old Town was only ten minutes from our house, but the air tasted different here.

"Did you come to help me or to pick up girls?" After the way the lady behind the register looked at me, I was pretty sure I wouldn't be a future employee of Urban Chic. *Perfectly fine with me.* There were so many sequins reflecting the fluorescent lighting in that store, I was sure it would produce a massive headache after five minutes.

"I can do both at the same time," he assured me. "I'm talented like that."

The only reason I chose Old Town to look for a place of possible employment was because it had so many stores so close together and I wouldn't have to drive all around town picking up applications. And unlike the mall, hopefully nobody I knew would come around. It was near the beach, so mostly tourists or rich types shopped here. The stores consisted mainly of local owners with local wares—lots of antique shops and vintage clothing stores. And although I liked the feel of the area, what I truly and sincerely hoped was that I wouldn't be able to find a job. Maybe that was why I stayed in my jeans and T-shirt, my hair pulled up into a ponytail, still wet from my shower.

"Never date a guy whose jeans don't cover his ankles," Gage said, pointing to the guy twenty yards ahead. He shuddered.

"But he'd be able to walk through puddles and stuff without even getting his jeans wet. He's a planner."

I often wondered why my brothers insisted on making these lists for me. It wasn't like I had been waiting anxiously on the sidelines for the dating buzzer to sound.

He laughed then steered me to the right. "That looks like a good store." So far Gage's employment suggestions had been influenced by whether there was a girl in the vicinity. This store just happened to have an outdoor fountain where a girl and her little sister (maybe?) were throwing spare change into the water.

"Do you think there's two hundred and sixty-four dollars' worth of change in there?" I watched the coins ripple the surface. "I could just come here once a week and collect the money out of the fountains."

"Now you're thinking creatively," Gage said. "I could totally get behind that idea." Then he cleared his throat and spoke a little louder. "My *sister*"—he always made sure hot girls knew our relationship—"and I were just trying to guess how much money is in this fountain."

"A million dollars," the little girl said.

"See, there you go," Gage said, looking at me. "Problem solved."

The dark-haired girl in low-rise jeans playfully hit her sister's shoulder and batted her eyelashes at Gage with a giggle. Before I hurled, I stepped into the store behind her and looked around.

The store smelled like old people—like books and bread and perfume. It was full of . . . stuff—mirrored boxes, colorful lamps, small dog statues. Did people buy small dog statues?

A girl, her blond hair tipped with pink, stood arranging knickknacks on a shelf.

"Hi. Could I get an application?" I asked.

"Of course." She walked to the counter and pulled a paper from beneath it. "We're not really hiring right now, but it doesn't hurt to try, right?"

"Right."

She bit her lip. "There's a store two doors down. A little clothing store owned by a lady named Linda. You should try there. Tell her Skye Lockwood sent you."

"Okay, thanks. I'm Charlie."

"Good to meet you."

I waved and walked out of the store.

"How'd it go?" Gage asked.

"Not hiring."

"Bummer. Well, I've already scored three phone numbers, so at least one of us is accomplishing something today."

"Thank you. Very motivating." I pointed up the way. "The girl told me to try some clothing store two doors this way, though."

We walked down the sidewalk and passed a doll store. "Oh, you so need to go in there," Gage said. I noticed the girl working inside was beautiful—of course. Next time I went job hunting I was leaving my brother at home. He opened the door and a bell announced our arrival. When we stepped in, I realized this store was either on the verge of closing or on the verge of opening. Boxes lay open all over the floor and were being packed . . . unpacked?

"Oh," she said when she saw us. "Hi. Sorry, we're closed. Xander must've left the door unlocked." She handed us a card. "But if you're looking for a doll, that's our website. We're going mobile."

"Mobile?" Gage asked.

"As in trade shows, fairs." She continued putting newspaper into a box.

"You need some help packing up?" Gage asked.

I grabbed Gage by the arm and yanked him out of the store.

"Did you see her eyes?" He put his hand over his heart and took a few staggering steps.

I rolled mine. "Last store," I said, pointing at the clothing store Skye must've been referring to. "Then I'm ready for food or something."

"I'll wait out here." When he said it, he gestured to a dance studio next door. A girl who looked about our age was inside, practicing in front of the mirrors.

"I swear, Gage. You're such a guy." I yanked open the door. The shop appeared free of any breathing person. It smelled like burning incense, but I couldn't find the source. There were a few headless mannequins wearing tiny dresses. Circular racks of clothes filled the middle of the store and more racks lined the walls. Along the back were large hutches housing small glass bottles. I couldn't tell if they were for sale or just on display. A floor lamp draped with a scarf stood unlit in the corner.

"Hello?" I called out. No answer. Just as I turned to leave, a middle-aged woman came out of the back room holding a coffee cup. Her brightly colored shirt looked straight out of India and her legs were clad in a wide-legged pair of dark jeans.

"Oh. Hello there." She set her cup down on the counter, put her palms together, and bowed. "Welcome."

"Okay. Thanks."

She stepped forward and I could see that her feet were bare. "How can I serve you?"

Was this lady for real? I tried to remember the name of the store I was in. Crazy Lady Central? Had I accidentally walked into a spiritual healing or massage therapy store? The mannequins and racks of clothes would seem to indicate otherwise, but I was no fashion expert.

I held up the papers already in my hand. "I just wanted to pick up an application. Um . . . Skye Lockewood said you might be hiring."

"Did she now? I don't have applications. It's just me. This is my store."

"Okay. Well, thanks anyway." I started to leave.

"But," she said as I was almost out the door, "I asked for a sign today and here you are."

"A sign?" I glanced out the window, hoping Gage would come in and save me. He was leaning against the glass next door staring inside dreamily. No help whatsoever. "I . . ." I took a step back. "Have a good day."

"You want a job, right?"

Not really. "Yes."

"Well, I've been contemplating expanding, bringing in new business. And if Skye vouches for you, maybe you're just the girl I've been waiting for."

I didn't tell her that Skye had just met me. "I'm pretty sure I'm not the girl anyone has been waiting for. I have no experience, I've never used a register in my life. I really wouldn't be very good selling clothes either. I mean, look at me."

She did. She took in my faded McKinley High T-shirt, my Target jeans, and my beat-up sneakers. "So you're looking for a job, but hoped you wouldn't find one? Let me guess. Parents forcing you to?"

"Yes. My dad."

"What's your name?"

"Charlie."

"Charlie, I'm Linda. I think I can give you the best deal in all of Old Town. From six to eight on Tuesdays and Thursdays and then four hours Saturday mornings. So what is that? Eight hours a week? Your dad will be appeased and you'll hardly have to work at all."

I nodded slowly. That didn't sound too bad. Even if it meant working with Crazy Barefoot Lady.

She moved to a small metal tree by the register where earrings hung and straightened a pair, then looked up at me expectantly.

"What's the pay?" In other words, how many weeks was it going to take me to pay off those tickets and get done with this?

"I can afford ten dollars an hour, so around a hundred and fifty dollars every two weeks, after taxes. But . . ."

Of course there's a catch.

"You would need to wear something more presentable. If you don't have anything, I will front you a paycheck to buy a few outfits, but then you'll be working those first two weeks for your clothes."

Ugh. Stupid clothes. I looked at the mannequins, who were showing more leg than I cared to see. "I don't do dresses."

"Of course not. I wouldn't put you in a dress like that anyway. It's all wrong for your aura."

My aura? I didn't know my aura had an opinion on dresses.

"What's today?" she asked.

"Wednesday."

"Okay, why don't you come in tomorrow before your shift starts and you can fill out some paperwork? Don't forget to bring your driver's license. . . . You are sixteen, right?"

"Yes."

"Good. Then after that I'll help you pick out a few things that would suit you."

Tomorrow. I'll have to start work tomorrow. "Okay."

She smiled, took a deep breath, then bowed again. "This feels right."

I nodded and backed my way out of the store. Was this what "right" felt like?

"How'd it go?" Gage asked.

"I got a job."

"Really?" He looked up at the name of the store. "Linda's Bazaar."

"Yeah."

"And was it bizarre?" He wiggled his fingers.

"You have no idea."

CHAPTER 5

• • • • • • •

My dad seemed surprised when I told him I'd gotten a job, like he'd expected me to come home a failure. I couldn't blame him. I was surprised too.

"Thanks for the vote of confidence, Dad."

"It's not that I didn't think you *could* get one, I just didn't think you really *would*."

"Yeah, yeah."

"Do you need anything?" He looked me up and down. "Uh . . . uniform or something?"

When I was with my brothers, my dad was perfectly normal, but when he singled me out, he was so awkward.

And always a beat behind. I still remembered when I was thirteen and my dad approached me one day. Sweat beaded his upper lip. "Charlie," he'd said, "Carol at work said you might need a bra." He said it so fast I almost didn't catch it. Then both of our faces reddened. "I could take you shopping," he added. "I guess they have stores where they help you get fitted . . . and stuff." My face still red, I assured him I already had a bra. I had learned the year before, when I started changing out for gym class, that everyone but me had one. I'd told my dad I needed money for cleats and used the money to buy one. Even though I hadn't known her, it was times like those that I longed for my mother.

"Linda—my new boss—she's going to help me get clothes."

He nodded, relieved. "Good. Good." Then he pulled me into a rare hug. "I'm proud of you." My dad was tall, so my cheek pressed against his chest. He smelled like cinnamon gum.

"No need to get all mushy. It's eight hours a week."

"I'm proud of you too," Gage said, throwing his arms around us and sending us all collapsing to the sofa.

"Gage," my dad grunted, untangling himself from our bodies and standing.

Gage filled in the now empty space by wrapping one arm around my neck and the other behind my knee and proceeding to fold me in half. I kicked and struggled to get out. "Surrender," he said.

"Don't break anything," my dad said and walked away. "Oh, and congratulations, Charlie."

"Thanks," I called, sounding a bit like Kermit the Frog with my neck bent over like that. I pinched Gage hard on the side and he yelped but didn't let go. I squirmed and kicked and wasn't above biting, but I couldn't get a good hold on his arm. My brothers always called me a cheater when I bit, but they had twice as much muscle as I did, so I had to find a way to even the playing field.

"Surrender," he said again.

I pushed off the ground with my free foot and almost succeeded in rolling us off the couch, but he eased me back into place.

"Charlie, you stubborn child, just admit I have you. You can't get out of this."

I pushed against his neck and he gagged a little, but then just pulled my arm into his hold. The front door opened and closed, and Braden said, "Hey, guys."

Gage looked over, distracted, and I forced my leg out of the hold then kneed him in the stomach. He reeled back and I jumped on him, pushing his face against the cushion.

"You're ruthless," he said.

"I learned it from you." I let him go, then stood.

"Hey, Braden. How was your mom's birthday dinner last night?"

"Same old, same old."

I tilted my head, wanting him to go on. Braden was an only child, so he was always the center of attention . . . and expectations. Sometimes I felt like he came to our house as often as he did to be surrounded by chaos. To disappear. I stared at him, but he didn't continue. He grabbed the remote off the end table and turned on the TV. "I thought for sure you guys would be watching the A's game."

"Whoa! What time is it?" I consulted the clock on the DVD player. "Crap. It's already halfway over." I claimed my position on the couch.

It was as if the sounds of the game called my brothers from their hideouts, because soon the living room was full, everyone shouting at the TV, soda cans and chips open on the coffee table. We didn't have a favorite sport in our house. We liked them all.

My dad came down and gestured for Gage to scoot over, which meant I had to scoot over into Braden's hard side. He moved his arm to the back of the couch to make more room. The smell of his deodorant assaulted my senses. "You smell good."

He pulled me into a headlock, holding me there for a minute. "You're stuck now."

I opened my mouth, ready to bite, when he must've realized what I was doing because he pushed me away with a laugh. I threw both my legs over one of Gage's and grabbed the jar of peanuts off the coffee table.

"No!" Braden yelled at the television, right in my ear. I elbowed him.

"Sorry," he said, distracted.

Gage absently patted one of my knees with his closed fist. *Thump thump thump.* I kicked a little and he stopped. But then Braden, drinking a soda, gulped loudly in my ear. Seriously, was he the loudest swallower in the world? I stood and started collecting empty soda cans off the table in front of us.

Braden reached up and pushed me over a little so he could see the TV.

"Oh, excuse me, was I in your way?"

"Yes, actually, so move it or lose it."

"Lose what?"

He pushed on the back of my knee with his foot and my leg gave out from under me, causing me to fall, the soda cans landing on the floor.

"Death to you."

I dropped to my hands and knees on the floor and collected the soda cans, then carried them toward the kitchen. As I reached the door, I looked over my shoulder. All their eyes were glued to the television. Warmth surged through my cold heart. I loved these guys so much. They were my life and I couldn't think of anything better than all of us together, just hanging out and doing nothing. I must have lingered in my happy feelings for too long, because Braden looked up, met my eyes, then gave me the "What's your deal?" face: one eyebrow raised, mouth twisted up.

I scrunched my nose at him and then walked into the kitchen.

CHAPTER 6

• • • • • • •

I hoped so badly that the guys never, ever came to visit me at work. This was my wish the next day as I stood in front of what had to be the most awful mirrors in the world—they showed three angles simultaneously—trying on the bajillionth outfit for Linda. I looked ridiculous.

We were behind some large flowered screens at the back of the store, so at least people walking by on the street outside couldn't witness my humiliation.

"These clothes fit you well," she said, adjusting the flowing top that hung a little too low in the front for my taste. I was used to the high neck of a T-shirt. And

I always thought jeans were meant for comfort. These jeans felt like they were attempting to hold my thighs in place.

"This is why models are so tall. Because clothes look good on tall people. It's completely unfair."

"Okay, I think I'm done playing dress-up forever. Which ones do you want me to buy?"

"Well, that's up to you, Charlie. Which ones speak to you?"

I coughed as I got a big whiff of the incense she had lit for this "experience." I waved my hand through the air. "Not a single piece of clothing spoke to me."

She placed a finger on my forehead. One thing I was learning rather quickly about Linda was that she didn't understand the concept of personal space. Not that I had a lot of personal space in my life, but generally strangers granted me that much. "Find your center. Feel your aura," she said, her finger still on my head.

"Neither me nor my aura know how to pick out clothes. Which ones do you like?"

"Okay. That's very practical of you. We are never fair judges of ourselves. An outside observer is much more likely to accurately tell us what looks the best on us." She studied all the clothes I had tried on.

A movement to my right caught my eye and I looked over.

"Mama Lou, how old is this Chinese food?" Skye, the girl with the pink-tipped hair who had referred me to Linda, walked out from the back room, holding up a container and tilting it so we could see the noodles inside. I didn't even know she was here. "Oh. Hi, Charlie. Cute outfit." She pointed at me with a fork.

I tugged on the bottom of the uncomfortable shirt, wondering if it was see-through. The material felt so thin. "Thanks."

Linda looked up in surprise. "Skye. When did you get here?"

"Just now. I came in the back door." She plopped down on a red circular ottoman next to the mirrors and lifted a forkful of noodles.

"I'm not sure how old that food is. At least a few days."

Skye sniffed it, then put it in her mouth.

Linda started separating the clothes I had tried on into two piles. "To buy now." She pointed at one pile. "To buy later." She nodded toward the other. Then she looked at the outfit still on my body. The mirror in front of me assured me the top wasn't see-through, but it felt so light. And it had a flower pattern on it. I could confidently say that I had never worn anything with flowers on it before. Well, maybe when I was five.

"And to wear now," she said, referring to the outfit I wore.

"Uh . . . I don't know that my aura is ready to jump right in with flowers."

She laughed like I was kidding but then threw me a striped shirt, which I changed into quickly.

"Let me ring this stuff up, then you can start work."

It felt like I had been hard at work for the last hour trying on those clothes. It was exhausting, and I hoped I never had to do it again. I checked myself out in the mirror again. I didn't look like me.

"You look great," Skye assured me through a mouthful of noodles.

When I came out from behind the screens Linda smiled. "So nice." She sighed like she had just performed some miracle and was pleased with the results. At least, until her gaze reached my face and hair. I could tell she wanted to say something, but it was one thing to tell someone to change her clothes; it was a whole other thing to tell someone her face could use some work.

She positioned herself behind the register, and I watched as the number on the tiny black screen got bigger and bigger.

"Skye," Linda called. "I got some more colored dye in."

Skye leaped off her low stool and headed for the hutch in the corner. "Green. Nice. I'm coming back after closing so you can help me."

Linda helped her dye her hair? Skye's parents must've been really laid-back. Well, Skye looked older than I was. Maybe she didn't live with her parents.

Linda tucked the receipt into her drawer, probably so she could deduct it from my paycheck later. "Sounds good," she said. "So scoot on out of here. I need to train Charlie now."

"Fine. Fine." Skye headed toward the back, and a thought suddenly occurred to me.

"Are you and Skye related?"

"Oh, no. Her mother left when she was young." A look of pity passed over Linda's face as she gazed toward the back of the store where Skye had just left. "She just needs an extra helping of love. That's all."

My breath caught. Is that how Linda saw the motherless of the world? Lacking somehow? I didn't say anything, but I didn't need to. Linda filled the silence by showing me how to fold shirts, organize racks by sizes, and properly hang pants.

The two hours went by pretty fast, and I changed back into my normal clothes, then collected my bag of new clothes and my car keys. Linda said, "So, I'll see you Saturday at ten a.m., Charlie." She paused, thoughtful. "Is that a nickname?"

"Short for Charlotte. But Charlie fits me better."

"It does." She pointed to the bag of clothes. "You

can wear them home, you know. They're completely machine-washable."

"Oh, yeah . . ." I shrugged my shoulders. "If my brothers saw me in these clothes, they'd never let me live it down."

"We live in our own minds, child."

Not in my house. In my house, we were always getting in each other's heads. It was hard enough keeping the guys out without giving them extra ammo. "I guess."

She had a set of keys in her hands and she followed me to the door, obviously about to lock up. "What about your mom? I'm sure she'd love to see you in those clothes."

That look of pity Linda had given when talking about Skye's motherless state flashed through my mind. I knew that look well. I'd seen it before. It was the look that always came after the line *My mom died when I was six.* That was my go-to line. That was usually followed by an apology from the listeners and then the look. Sometimes the look lingered for months, every time they saw me. It was hard to say which was worse: the look, or when the look finally went away, the memory of my story fading into the recesses of their minds. How could they forget when I couldn't?

I hadn't seen that look directed at me in a while. Most people just knew. We lived in the same house and went to the same schools pretty much my whole life.

I opened my mouth to avoid the question when "My mom's like me. She doesn't know a thing about fashion" came out. My face flushed hot and I stepped outside without turning back. Did I really just pretend my mom was alive? Not only that, I gave her *my* fashion sense. I knew that wasn't even true. I'd seen enough pictures of her to know she always looked gorgeous. The picture my mind always went to was my mom in a long yellow sundress, standing on the beach looking out at the waves.

But I didn't know much outside of pictures. I used to ask my dad questions about her, but as I got older I noticed the sad looks that accompanied the answers and stopped asking. I stopped asking long before I could start asking questions that really mattered. I wondered if I'd ever get the motivation or courage to start asking again.

CHAPTER 7

• • • • • • •

It was the first night in a long time that I woke up with a start. My hands shook, and I clenched them into fists, then crossed my arms over my chest to try and stop the quivering there as well.

The nightmare always began the same, my mother tucking me into bed, kissing my forehead, and saying good-bye. Rain pounded the window as if trying to make her stay, my heart seeming to keep up with the rapid pattering. After that it was a variation. Sometimes it was a car accident, her car sliding off the side of a road and down an embankment. That nightmare made sense because it was what had actually happened. As such, it was the one I had the most often.

But sometimes there were different versions altogether: hands made of rain ripping my mother from where she stood in my bedroom doorway, instantly liquefying her; a strong wind tearing the roof off our house and sucking her into the night. Tonight she had stood in front of our house, in white pajamas, and the rain itself had sliced bloody cuts down her body until she collapsed to the wet grass, her white nightdress now red, her limp hand filling my view as I stared at its lifelessness.

My new job had deprived me of my late afternoon run, leaving my body less exhausted than normal. I'd have to figure out a new running schedule for Tuesdays and Thursdays. My dad didn't like me to run alone at night, and it wasn't often I could talk one of my brothers into going with me.

I lay there staring at the ceiling, wondering what my brain would do to me if I fell back asleep. Late the next morning, we were supposed to play a game of basketball on the elementary school's outdoor blacktop. I wished it were morning already.

My clock read three a.m., and my now frayed nerves weren't letting me go to sleep. I rolled out of bed and walked downstairs. First I paced the kitchen, then I went outside. Before I discovered the amazing effects of running four years earlier, I spent a lot of hours in the stillness of my backyard.

I walked the cement around the pool, staring down at the dark water as I did.

A set of headlights swept across the blackness as Mr. Lewis's truck pulled up next door. I was surprised at how late he was getting home. Lights went on upstairs a few minutes later, and that's when the yelling started.

I backed up to get a better view of the upstairs. A few more lights flipped on, and then the back door slammed shut. Peering through the cracks of the fence that separated our houses, I saw Braden emerge wearing a pair of boxers and a hastily thrown-on T-shirt, all twisted at the bottom.

"Psst," I called through the fence. "Braden."

He looked around and then straight at the fence, not able to see me, but obviously knowing it was someone in the general vicinity.

"Gage?" he asked.

"No, it's Charlie. What's going on?"

He walked closer. "Where are you?"

I held my hand above the fence, then he walked straight to me. "You okay?"

He sat down and leaned his back against the boards. I did the same. "My dad just came home . . . drove home . . . drunk out of his mind. I almost wish your dad had seen him driving so he could've hauled him in."

"Why does he feel the need to wake you and your mom up when he's like that?"

"Because apparently he remembers everything he hates about us when he's drunk and has an overwhelming desire to share his feelings."

"That sucks." The night was warm, and I let it fill my lungs. I pulled on a string hanging off the bottom of my cotton pants. "So you come outside when he's like this?"

"Usually. I find that if I walk away he eventually cools down. My mom still hasn't learned that lesson after all these years."

We went quiet, leaving only the sound of muffled yelling coming from his house. "Is she . . . he won't hurt her . . . will he?"

"No," Braden said darkly.

I leaned my head back against the fence. His parents either went to bed or stopped screaming because I couldn't hear them anymore.

Braden's voice was lighter when he asked, "And what brings you out on this fine evening?"

"Couldn't sleep."

"Really? The soundest sleeper in the universe couldn't sleep? Why?"

"Stupid job messed with my schedule. I didn't get a chance to run tonight."

"Oh yeah, the job. I heard about this miraculous event. How did it go?"

"It was sheer torture. I'm counting down the days

until I earn the five hundred bucks necessary to be done with this sentence."

"Didn't your dad say something about a hundred bucks a month after that too, though? For insurance or something?"

I groaned. "You're right. I guess I'll have to earn another couple hundred and hope I can plea-bargain after that. I think when school starts, that will be a huge argument against having a job."

"I'm sure you'll figure out something."

Stillness took over for a while, and just when I started to think he'd fallen asleep there against the fence, he said, "You playing ball tomorrow?"

"Of course. You?"

"Yeah. Are you playing for the team this year at school?"

I nodded, even though he couldn't see me. "Uh-huh. Can't wait for it to start. Talk about exhaustion. School, basketball, gym, homework, bed—now that's a schedule my body likes."

"Why?"

Crap. The problem with talking to his disembodied voice was that it made me less guarded. It didn't feel like I was talking to anyone but the sky. "I just like to sleep good. None of this waking-up-at-three-a.m. crap."

"*Heck* yeah," he said in his best imitation of me (which

wasn't very good). Every time I substituted a bad word with a milder one, he made fun of me by doing his own bad-to-less-bad word substitution. His taunts weren't going to pressure me into changing things. I was more scared of my dad's no-cussing rule than I was of Braden laughing at me for it.

"I knew you were going to say that," I said.

"Oh, really? You knew I was going to say 'Heck yeah'?"

"Well, some variation of it."

"You think you know me so well, huh?"

"Yep. Every last annoying habit."

He gave a single laugh. "Well, it goes both ways. Actually, I probably know you better."

"You think you know me better than I know you?"

"Yes," he said confidently. "Because I see you every day, and when I don't see you, I hear Gage talk about whatever lame thing you guys did."

"And you don't think Gage talks about all the lame things you guys do without me?"

"Okay, game on." That was his competition voice. As he said it, I realized I knew it so well. His voice in general was so familiar to me. I was surprised I could picture his expressions as I listened to him talk. Right now he'd have a smug smile on his face. "We will prove who knows more about the other. We go back and forth stating facts. Whoever runs out first loses."

"You're on. I'll start. You have swampy brown eyes."

He laughed. "Oh, wow, you're really starting with the basics."

"Yep. I said I knew everything. That's part of every-thing." The truth was, I wasn't sure I did know everything about Braden. As Gage's best friend, he was as familiar to me as a brother, but in some ways, he was a mystery to me. But I assumed I was the same for him, so I had con-fidence that I knew him at least as well as he knew me.

"Swampy? Really? You make them sound nasty."

"Yes, they are swampy." His eyes were awesome— brown interlaced with green. It was like they couldn't quite decide which color team they wanted to play for. "Your turn."

"Fine. You have steel-gray eyes."

"Oh, I see how you are. Stealing my facts."

"Yeah, we should be able to match the other person's fact. If I didn't know your eye color and you knew mine, I should've lost right there. So now you have to match my fact."

I nodded. "Okay. I get it. Evolving rules. So you're up then."

"Right. You suck at math."

I gasped in mock offense. "Rude . . . but true." Okay, so I needed to think of a subject in school Braden was bad in. Problem. Braden was an excellent student. So my match could've been that he didn't suck at any subject, but I didn't want to praise him after he just slammed me. "Oh! Got it. You suck at choir. Supporting evidence: You volunteer for the solo in the seventh grade Christmas program. You forget the song. You sing the few words you remember completely off-key." I laughed, remembering the cringe-worthy moment. "I think we still have that on home video somewhere."

"Ouch." He probably grabbed his chest then, but he had at least half a smile on his face. Braden was good at crooked smiles. "For the record, your brother volunteered me for that solo when I was absent and I beat him for it after the fact. But yes, I suck at choir."

"My turn," I said, conjuring up a mental picture of Braden so I could think of my next fact. I almost said he had a scar through his right eyebrow, but that suddenly seemed so personal. Maybe I shouldn't know that about him. Especially since it was barely noticeable. "You hate to lose."

"That's a wash."

"What do you mean?"

"I mean, so do you, so those facts cancel each other out. Well, actually, you *really* don't like to lose and I just sort of don't like to lose, so you're probably right. I should probably think of something you just sort of don't like."

"Whatever, punk! You know you hate to lose as much

as I do. And the proof of that will come when I beat you at this game and you cry like a baby."

The arguing renewed in his house and we both fell silent. He sighed. "I guess I should probably go back inside and try to steer him toward sleep."

"Does that work?"

"Sometimes."

"Good luck."

"Yeah." After he walked a few shuffling steps away, I heard him whisper, "This isn't over. I will beat you."

"Never," I said with a smile.

The next morning when Braden walked in the back door and through the kitchen, where I sat eating breakfast, we both pretended the night before hadn't happened. I picked up the basketball I had been propping my feet on and threw it at the back of his head as he walked by. He turned around and walked back to where I sat at the bar. He smeared his finger across the top of my peanut butter toast and then stuck the big glob in his mouth as he walked away.

"Gross," I called after him. I wasn't sure why we'd both decided to pretend it didn't happen, but I was relieved he didn't mention the late-night chat by the fence. It almost made it seem like it took place in a different reality.

CHAPTER 8

• • • • • • •

Saturday morning at work was busier than I would've liked, but I didn't see anyone I knew, so that was good. Linda taught me to use the register, and by Tuesday she had the nerve to leave me alone for an hour while she had dinner. I told her if I gave away all the money in the register it was all on her. She told me she trusted me and my math abilities. I didn't mention that I sucked at math.

Thirty minutes into my alone time with the register, Skye came running in from the back. Her hair was now platinum blond with streaks of green. She had on a flowy, robelike shirt, much like one of the shirts Linda had me buy that I hadn't dared to wear yet, and was holding a pair of boots in her hand, calling, "Mama Lou!" She slid to a stop on the hardwood floor and looked at me. "Hi, Charlie. Where's Linda?"

"Eating."

Her shoulders slumped. She held up one of the boots. "Do you see that?"

I wasn't exactly sure what she wanted me to see. I obviously saw the big black boot she held up, so there must've been some detail about it I was supposed to notice, but for the life of me I didn't see anything but a boot. "Uh . . . no?"

"I tried on the left boot at the thrift store. This is the right boot. I didn't even notice it was missing two lace hooks right in the middle. A total rookie mistake."

I smiled at her use of a sports analogy.

"You don't know how to fix it, do you?"

I still didn't even know what she was talking about. "Duct tape?"

She laughed.

"Linda can fix shoes?"

"I don't know. She always has some creative solution for my problems. How long has she been gone?"

"About thirty minutes."

"Maybe I'll wait." She wandered over to a hutch and started squirting herself with a glass bottle that I thought was just for show.

I straightened some hanging shirts. "I think I saw you

the other day, walking with someone holding a guitar case."

"Henry. My boyfriend. He plays for a local band. Well, I shouldn't call them local anymore—they're getting some statewide gigs. It's pretty amazing. They still play here sometimes, though." She picked up a different glass bottle and walked over to me. "Can I use your arm? I don't want to mix scents."

I held up my arm and she twisted it, palm up, then sprayed a small amount on my wrist.

She put her arm next to mine. "You're tan."

"My mother was Mexican." I bit down on my tongue, hoping she didn't catch the *was* I threw in there. I didn't want to have to explain that word. Especially not when I kind of told Linda my mother was alive.

"Ah. Well, that makes sense." She smiled, then smelled my wrist and curled her lip. "No on that scent." She replaced the bottle, then sighed. "I think I will try the duct tape idea after all. It could look really good with these boots."

"Will you be able to get them off?"

She laughed. "Eventually." She headed toward the back.

I wondered why she always came that way. She obviously had a key, but if she was coming from her shop a couple of doors down, wouldn't it be just as easy to walk in the front door?

"Thanks for the good idea, Charlie." She paused for a moment. "By the way, you look really cute."

She left, and I looked down at my outfit—a pair of jeans and a satiny black shirt with a little lace around the neckline. I had worn my tennis shoes in to work and Linda immediately called a friend, who brought over a pair of black sandals. Apparently I had committed a fashion foul with my shoes. All I cared about was that the sandals were super comfortable.

A while later, Linda came back into the store carrying a handful of colorful leaflets and ads.

"What are those?"

She spread them out on the counter next to the register. "Makeup ads." She held one up. "I think I'm going to carry some designer makeup in the store. A girl came by the other day and asked if I'd be interested. I think it will drum up some business. What do you think?"

"I have no opinion in these types of matters. I'm clueless. But I guess it can't hurt to offer a bigger variety of items."

"Exactly. Hopefully we'll get crossover traffic. I've been thinking about this for a while now. The girl is going to come in and do a demonstration. She's thinking about offering weekly makeup classes to draw people in. You get to be her blank canvas for the class."

She said it so casually that I didn't catch the meaning at first.

When I realized what she'd said, my hand froze above the ad it had been reaching for. "Wait, what?"

"You'll just have to sit there. You won't even have to say a word."

"No way. Nuh-uh. You should have Skye do it. She was just in here a little while ago."

"I would, but Skye works on Saturdays. Plus, I think you'd be better at it."

"In what universe? No way."

She took a breath and then closed her eyes. Holding her hands about an inch from her body, she ran them from her head to her waist, then opened her eyes like nothing had happened. "Just think on it. I will give you a split commission for whatever we make from the class." She swooshed her hands back and forth in front of me as though clearing away some invisible dust, hoping to give her idea a clear lane to my brain. "Just think on it." She handed me one of the makeup pamphlets.

Back home, I walked the path up to the house, staring at the girl on the front. She was coated in makeup. More makeup than I had ever seen on a face in real life. It did not look pleasant to me at all. I sighed and opened the door.

A Nerf gun was shoved into my hand, and Braden grabbed me by the arm and pulled me into the dark front room, pushing me up against the wall. "You are now on my team," he whispered, no more than two inches from my face. A piece of his reddish-brown hair flopped into his eye and he pushed it back. "Three shots equal death." He grabbed the pamphlet and the bag full of my work clothes out of my hand and flung them onto the couch five feet away. The makeup ad didn't quite make it and fluttered to the ground in front of the couch.

"You ready?" he asked, stepping back in front of me. He was so close that his hip brushed against my side. A chill went through me.

He tilted his head and his face moved closer to mine. I froze. Then he sniffed my hair and neck. "What's that smell?"

For a second I couldn't answer him. My breath seemed caught in my throat. Then I held up my wrist, between our too-close faces, "It's a spray from work. A girl, Skye, she sprayed it on me." My voice came out tight and I let my hand fall back to my side.

Braden lowered his brow. "What's wrong?" he said. His eyes flickered to my lips, then back to my eyes.

My heart picked up speed. What was going on? I put my arms between our chests, needing a little space. Work was making me weird, I decided. Linda, with all her talk of auras and makeup and fashion, was not good for me. "Nothing." I looked over his shoulder to the shadowy hall, sure my brothers would've heard us by now. We were probably about to get ambushed. "Who's playing?"

"Everyone."

"My dad?"

"No. He's at work."

I slipped off my shoes so I could be stealthier, hooked my arm in his, and crept along the wall. "We are so winning."

Braden smiled big. "I knew I made the right choice holdin' out for you to get home."

"Darn straight."

"Let's kick some *butt*," he said, in his horrible imitation of me.

A low voice from across the hall said, "I could've killed you guys three times by now. Stop flirting with my sister and get your head in the game. I'll give you a ten-second head start."

His accusation made my heart jump. But this was Gage. He was always joking. Plus, he never stopped flirting. Ever. He probably just assumed the same of everyone else. "Shut up," I said, then pulled Braden the opposite way down the hall. Ten seconds wasn't very long.

CHAPTER 9

• • • • • • •

That night in my room I stared at the girl in the ad some more. Makeup wasn't so bad. It wasn't practical with sports—sweat and makeup did not mix well—but I'd worn mascara on occasion. And ChapStick was my best friend. The extra money helping Linda out with this project sounded great to put a dent in what I owed my dad so I could quit this job faster. But there was no way I'd come home with my face caked in the stuff. I'd never hear the end of it. I sighed and shoved the ad in my desk drawer.

★ ★ ★

I walked in to work Thursday, set the pamphlet on the counter in front of Linda, and said, "It's not waterproof, right?"

"What?"

"The makeup. I want to be able to wash it off easily when I'm finished."

"I bet your mom would love to see you all made up."

This was why it wasn't good to lie. I'd honestly thought the subject would never come up again. This was way worse than the pity looks she would've given me. I shrugged.

She looked back at the ad. "It will come off easily with a good face wash."

I nodded slowly, still not sure I wanted to do this. "And I won't have to talk?"

She threw her hands in the air in an excited gesture like she thought I'd made up my mind. "No. Just a canvas. It will be great. She'll do the first class this Saturday morning." She pulled a form out from beneath the counter, proving she knew I would agree. "Because you're underage, I need your mother—well, either of your parents—to sign this consent form. For liability issues. Amber isn't licensed, which is why she isn't putting makeup on anyone but you during the class. And also, I'm not worried about it, but if you have some sort of allergic reaction, this says you won't sue me."

I nodded and took the form, my eyes scanning over the words but not reading them.

"You should tell your mom to come watch."

Every time she mentioned my mother, my stomach tightened. I should just tell her the truth and get it over with. Instead the words "My mom has to work Saturday so she won't be able to make it" came out. My mouth had a mind of its own lately. I held up the form. "But I'll get this signed."

"Sounds good. Let's get to work."

That night I couldn't sleep for two reasons: one, because I hadn't run, and two, because the paper that I had forged my dead mother's signature on screamed at me. It sat in my desk drawer, yelling at the top of its lungs. I should've just asked my dad to sign it. He would've . . . probably. After asking lots of questions.

I remembered one time my dad came home with a bottle of conditioner and put it on the desk in front of me. "Do you need this? Carol at work said you might." I stared at the bottle. Of course I knew what it was, I'd seen enough commercials, but I had never used it before. He had guilt in his eyes like he had somehow failed me. It wasn't his fault he didn't know. It would've been so much easier if he had four boys. I knew that, and I knew he knew that. "No, I'm good. My hair doesn't really get that tangled. But thanks. I'll use it." And I did. I couldn't believe I had lived that long without it.

I wondered if he'd feel just as guilty now for not buying me makeup. I sighed and stared at my desk as if the form Linda gave me was going to burn its way through the drawer. I finally rolled out of bed at one a.m. and turned on the lamp on my nightstand. What was wrong with me? I had justified the act by telling myself that the release was just a formality. I wasn't going to have an allergic reaction, so it was unnecessary. And my dad would never find out. It wasn't like this paper would be sent to the government to check and verify. It would get filed away in the ugly metal desk in the stockroom at Bazaar, never to be pulled out again.

I made my way downstairs. Once in the kitchen, I had a clear view of Braden's house. His bedroom light was on. I grabbed my phone and texted him. *Up for a fence chat?*

Yep.

"Hey," he said when we stood separated by the wooden barrier.

"Hi." I waited for him to talk first, even though I was the one who'd called him out here. I felt embarrassed by the rashness of that decision. Instead of facing the fence, staring at his shadowy figure through the slats, I adopted our previous pose of sitting, back to the fence, then looked up at the moon. It was so much easier to talk to the moon than to Braden. At least about real stuff. I listened as he did the same thing.

"So, you're up late tonight," I said.

"Yeah." He offered no explanation.

My neck hurt, and I rubbed at it. "Have you ever done something stupid and then felt incredibly guilty about it?"

"Yes." Again, he didn't expound. "What did you do?"

Pretended my life was whole. "Lied."

"To who?"

"My boss."

"About?"

"About . . ." Why did the moon make me want to spill all my secrets to Braden? ". . . something really dumb, but now I don't know how to tell her the truth."

"What's your boss like?"

"Weird. I think she took one of those spiritual journeys around the world or something and thinks she's reached some sort of inner peace. Now her self-imposed job in life is to fix broken spirits."

Braden sometimes pulled on his bottom lip when he was thinking, and I could hear that he was doing that when he said, "And she thinks your spirit is broken?"

The clouds around the moon glowed white. "No. Not mine. Well, yes, mine, but not just mine, everyone's. She thinks everyone has a broken spirit."

"Everyone but her."

"Yes, exactly."

"So you lied to keep her out of your personal business?"

"Yes."

"Then stop worrying about it. She doesn't need to butt into your life anyway. If it's nothing big then just forget about it."

I just reincarnated a dead person, that's all, nothing big. "Yeah, you're probably right."

"Is that a first?"

"What?"

"Me being right?"

"Ha. Ha." And then it was quiet. So quiet I could hear his breaths, deep and long. With each breath, it seemed, my shoulders relaxed.

"But if it is something big . . ." He trailed off and my shoulders immediately tensed again. "It will just eat at you."

I knew this was true. It was already making a meal of my insides. "Well, as long as it starts with some of my more useless organs, then I have some time."

He laughed.

"You eat a lot of carrots."

"Uh . . . what?"

"You like carrots. That's my fact about you. You know, in the game of proving I know more about you and your boring life than you know about mine."

"But carrots aren't my favorite food." He'd sounded smug when he said it, like he was announcing I had lost.

"I didn't say they were. I said you eat a lot of them. Maybe they're not listed next to 'Favorite Food' in your 'My Favorite Things' diary entry, but you like them."

"No, they're listed next to 'Favorite Vegetable.'"

"I knew it."

"Okay, my match . . . You are forever eating Cocoa Krispies. Loudly."

"It's a loud cereal."

We spent the next several minutes listing off the other items that were in our fictitious Favorite Things diary entries. His: color—blue, subject—history, food—steak, and day—Saturday. Mine: red, PE, pizza, and Friday (previously Saturday until work butted in).

"I have one," he announced. "You hate girls who wear sparkly words across their butts."

I laughed. "How could you possibly know that?" I had never said that pet peeve out loud.

"Because I see the look on your face when a girl with the word *juicy* on her butt is walking in front of us. It's pretty funny."

"Yes, it's true. I'm not a fan." I raised a finger in the air even though he couldn't see me. "Never date a girl who feels the need to make her butt a billboard."

He gave a little humming noise.

"What?"

"I think that's the first time you've ever given an opinion about who I should date. What else should I avoid?"

"I don't know your type of girls, Braden." Girly girls were so far out of my circle of friends that I didn't even begin to try to understand them. "I have no idea what makes a girl undateable. Truthfully, I'm not even sure a girl with a sparkly announcement on her butt isn't worthy, seeing as how I've never spent more than one minute talking to a girl like that."

"I'm sure Gage will bring one home eventually, and then you can find out."

I laughed. "True."

"What did you mean by that, anyway?"

"By what?"

"That you don't know *my* type of girls?"

"I hang out with athletes."

"And?"

I paused, a little surprised. Was he saying he would date my teammates if I set him up? It had been a while since Braden had a girlfriend, but I was pretty sure his last one knew more about nail patterns than defensive patterns. "And . . . I guess I don't know your type."

He chuckled. "I find that hard to believe."

My cheeks prickled and goose bumps formed on my arms. I didn't let my mind follow that implication down any of the paths it seemed to want to go. That didn't mean anything. It really didn't. He just meant that I knew him well, so I knew exactly the type of girl he would date. And I did. One who did her hair and knew how to pick out cute clothes and didn't wear running shoes everywhere.

Braden cleared his throat. "Do you have a match for my fact, or did I win?"

It took me a minute to remember what his fact was. I had to backtrack to the sparkly-words-across-the-butt comment. "You honestly think you're going to win that easily?" So did his fact mean that in order to match I had to figure out something he hated about guys? I pictured Braden at school. Even though he was a jock he was fairly inclusive. "Okay, so since I don't really hate girls with the word *juicy* on their butts, I just think it's a poor fashion choice, I'm going to match with loafers."

"Loafers?"

"You think guys shouldn't wear loafers."

He gave a breathy laugh. "I'll give you credit for that one."

"But . . ."

"But what?"

"But it's not quite right. So if it's not poor fashion, what is it about loafers that you don't like?"

"It's not so much the loafers as it is the guys wearing the loafers."

"Oh, really?" That was news to me. "What about them?"

"They're usually rich, preppy snobs who think the world owes them something. Frat types."

"Wow, all that from a pair of shoes? Are you generalizing, Braden?"

"Maybe. Just be wary of useless shoes, Charlie. What someone wears on their feet says a lot about them."

I looked down at my bare feet and wiggled my toes. I wondered if that rule applied to girls, too, or just guys. "Noted. So no dating guys who drink V8, wear loafers or too-short jeans—"

"Who set the too-short jeans rule?"

"Gage."

"Good call." I could hear the smile in his voice when he said, "How many rules has he given you?"

"Too many. I don't remember half of them." Most of them were jokes, I knew, but it was hard to feel like any guy would ever measure up to my brothers' ridiculous guidelines.

"Don't worry, I've been keeping notes for you. I'll add that one to the list."

I laughed.

Braden let out a large yawn. "Okay. I better get to bed or you're going to school me in soccer tomorrow."

I smiled. Considering how crappy I felt when I came outside, I was surprised at how my insides seemed to soar. "Make sure you wear the right shoes."

"Always."

CHAPTER 10

• • • • • • •

"Here she comes." Linda pointed at the door and a girl who carried a bag big enough to hold ten soccer balls. That was all makeup? "She's a little chatty, by the way."

The door swung open, and the girl and her big bag came through it. She looked about my age. "Hello!" the girl said as she approached. "I almost got lost even though I've been here before and Old Town is tiny. For some reason I just thought you were past Fifth instead of Fourth and I was so turned around that I thought I was going to miss our time. I sent out a flyer and we should be packed this morning. I'm so excited. Where should I set up? That counter looks good. I'll just unload there. You have a backed stool like we talked about, right?"

A *little* chatty? She must've spoken at the rate of five hundred words a minute. She looked at me. "You must be Charlie. I'm Amber. Oh, look at you, you left yourself completely blank for me, no false lashes or anything. And I even get to shape your brows? This is going to be great." She stepped closer and studied my face. "You have the perfect skin and bone structure for this. We are going to sell lots of makeup today."

Did she have to breathe like the rest of us? Because I didn't hear a single breath during her speech. Deepsea divers could train themselves to hold their breath for seven minutes at a time. Were Olympic-caliber talkers the same way?

Linda laughed like she was very amused with Amber.

"So we have about thirty minutes before the class starts. If we move some of these racks of clothes off to the side, we could set up some chairs here in the middle. Did the chairs get delivered? I called yesterday to make sure they were set to arrive this morning, but I don't see them."

"They're in the back," Linda said.

"I'll start bringing them out." I needed a break. She was exhausting.

"Thank you so much. I'll get the makeup ready."

★ ★ ★

We weren't even five minutes into the class and I knew I never wanted to do it again. She was explaining to the group how to properly pluck eyebrows, and my face was raw from the pain. So far I had managed to keep from actually screaming out loud, but I wasn't sure if I could keep that up. My nose itched and my eyes watered.

"Charlie already has a very nicely shaped eyebrow, so we won't get carried away. Just a little cleaning up."

I wondered what a lot of cleaning up would feel like. I went into a zone, completely shutting out everything around me. My brain went through basketball plays, and my shoulders immediately relaxed. Five more weeks until camp, when I was sure my dad would let me quit this job. It just wouldn't be practical to keep it when I had to leave for a week and then start school right when I got back. He'd see the logic. Plus, by then, I'd have . . . I did the math in my head and knew I wouldn't have quite enough to cover my tickets. Still, he'd let me off. He had to.

It was hard to tell how much time passed. I guess I could've counted Amber's words and figured it out that way. She hadn't stopped talking the entire time. But at one point she stepped to the side and said, "And that is a daytime look with the Max line."

A couple of people said, "Ooh," and I didn't know if

that was a good or bad thing.

"Next week we'll showcase the evening look. There are order forms in your booklet, and please feel free to ask me any questions. Most of the products I have in stock. I'll also be setting up a display here in Bazaar, in case you can't buy all the things you have on your list today."

I wondered how long I had to sit there before I could go to the back and wash my face. My leg bounced and twitched as I waited. I'd already been sitting for way too long. A couple of people walked over to talk to Amber and pointed out different things on my face like I wasn't there. Not that I'd have been able to answer their questions, but it still felt weird.

Linda came over and patted my shoulder. "You did so well, and you look amazing."

I shrugged.

"Sit still for a minute, I'm going to grab my camera from the back so I can take a picture for your mom."

My stomach twisted with guilt.

When Linda left, Amber said, "Thanks, Charlie. You are the perfect canvas. Your features were made to show off makeup. I don't believe how enormous your eyes look with mascara."

And enormous eyes were a good thing?

Amber turned her attention to the line of people that

had formed, orders in hand, and began working her way through them. Linda came back out with the camera and took several pictures of me. "I'm going to print one of these off across the street. Watch the store for me."

"You really don't need to do that," I said.

But she waved her hand through the air and kept walking.

The line finally thinned and people clutching cute purple bags with tissue paper left the store, chatting. Amber said, "Don't forget to tell your friends, and come back for the evening face next week," as each of them walked away.

Two girls who looked as made-up as Amber joined us in front after everyone had left. "You did good, Amber."

"So, what do you think, girls? Easy, right? You guys could each find your own store. Maybe one of you can hit a downtown shop. This is definitely going to earn me enough for my fall wardrobe."

"So, Linda said you might have some good face wash for me?" I asked before she and her friends got too busy talking about clothes.

"You're going to wash it off?" one of them said.

"Well, I'm playing ball after this, so it's not really practical."

Amber smiled, reached into her bag, and pulled out a green package. "These are face wipes. You should need just one."

I took them. "Thanks."

"Oh, and if you want, Charlie, I'll give you all the makeup I used on you today at cost."

"Um . . . I haven't been paid yet."

She grabbed one of the thick catalogs of makeup, turned it to the front page where there was a picture of her, and circled her phone number. "Well, call me if you change your mind. I can deliver." She handed it to me.

Linda returned, and I pointed to the back. She nodded. I started to walk away.

"Charlie," Amber called. I turned around. "We're going out to lunch, the three of us." She pointed to her two friends. "Do you want to come?"

I couldn't think of anything worse than sitting with three girls I hardly knew and having to think of something to say. "I have plans today. Next time?"

"Next Saturday." She smiled. "I'm holding you to it."

As I walked away, I pulled out a wipe and started scrubbing my face immediately. When I got to the bathroom, I stopped in front of the sink. My breath caught when I saw myself in the mirror. The image reminded me of the picture hanging in our hallway—my mom on her wedding day. My heart clenched. I scrubbed faster.

"What are you doing?" Gage asked, barging into my room after a single knock.

I slammed the picture Linda had taken of me face-down on the table. "Nothing."

"Uh, okay. I'll leave it alone because I don't know if I want to know after a reaction like that."

"Yeah, you should. What do you want?"

He fell back onto my bed. "Tomorrow we're playing disc golf at Woodward Park. You in?"

"Of course." I looked at the clock. Ten. "Hey, will you go running with me?"

"When?"

"Right now."

"No, but thanks for asking."

"Thanks for nothing."

"It's ten o'clock. If I go run right now I'll be up all night."

If I don't *go run right now, I will be.* "Please, Gage. I'd love you forever."

"Hmmm, I'm pretty sure I already have that one locked down, but maybe a different bribe would work. Like showing me whatever that is." He pointed to the picture on my desk.

No. Way. "Yeah, not going to happen. I don't need to go running after all." I tucked the picture into my desk drawer.

"Huh. Really? Now it is my goal in life to find out what you're hiding."

"That's a pretty lame goal."

"True. But I have this tingly feeling right here"—he pointed to his heart—"that it will be worth it."

"Get out of here before I have to kick your butt."

On his way out he grabbed hold of my ponytail, pulling both me and my chair backward, then lowered the chair gently to the ground.

"You're an idiot," I said, staring up at him from my new position on my back.

Rain pounded my window. Red rain. So hard that a single crack formed at the top of the glass and slowly splintered down in a sharp line. I watched it, the white line splitting my window into equal parts. And then suddenly it shattered, sending glass spraying into my bedroom.

I sat up with a start.

If I could control my subconscious mind, I would never ever dream. There had to be some way to solve this problem. Hypnosis or something. Maybe just a treadmill. What were the odds my dad would buy me one of those?

Downstairs, I made some hot chocolate and turned on the laptop. I Googled *dream interpretation* and searched for the word *rain*. There was always rain in my dream. I read: *Falling rain is a metaphor for tears, crying, or sadness.*

Yeah, whatever. I couldn't remember the last time I cried. I looked up *recurring dreams.*

Dreams are messages, things our minds want us to learn. Recurring dreams can be really important messages. They often come in the form of nightmares. Recurring dreams could represent a real-life problem that hasn't been dealt with or resolved. Overcoming or resolving that problem could help one move past the recurring dream.

I read the paragraph again. What credentials did a stupid online dream interpreter have anyway? I could make up garbage like this. Closing the laptop, I moved to the back door and looked over at Braden's house. It was two a.m.; there was no way he was up again. It would be completely selfish to text him. I knew this, and yet I got my phone and stared at his name for a long time.

I put the phone down, deciding against it, and went outside. His bedroom window was dark. The whole house was dark. Maybe he'd come out on his own like he did the first time. That wouldn't be selfish of me. I craned my neck to see if his father's car sat in his driveway.

Wait.

I was hoping his dad would come home drunk and drive Braden outside? That was more selfish than if I just texted him.

"Sorry," I whispered. "I hope he never comes home

that way again." I placed my palm on the fence as if I had somehow just sent that message to Braden. Then I sat down on the dirt. It felt warm between my fingers. "I dream about my mom," I said to the moon. "How is it possible to miss someone I never knew?"

If Braden were out here, what would be my match? What did he dream about? Leaving this place? He was a year older than I was, like Gage. He'd be a senior this year. And then what? I knew in my heart he'd be gone as soon as he turned in his graduation robes. With a home life like his, what did he have to stay for? My heart sank with that thought. I hoped his friendship with our family, with Gage . . . with me, might keep him here.

CHAPTER 11

• • • • • • •

"I know how to play," I said, shaking Braden's hand off my arm. "Don't be all condescending with me."

"I'm just trying to help your technique, Charlie."

"I'm sorry, did you become a professional disc golf instructor and forgot to tell any of us?"

He grunted. "You're so stubborn."

"If I had asked for help, I would accept your help."

Jerom joined in. "That's the issue—you never ask for help."

"Because I don't need help. Now back up before I whack you all in the head with this."

Braden took a large, deliberate step back.

I analyzed the positions of the trees around us, hoping I didn't hit any of them and prove him right. Nature had provided plenty of obstacles in this park. A dog to our left barked and then ran past us chasing a tennis ball; its owner let out a whistle.

I shook off the distractions, stood up straighter, then threw the Frisbee. It landed within five feet of the basket. Way closer than where Braden's sat at least ten feet from mine. "So there."

He rolled his eyes like he wished Fate had taught me a lesson right then and he was frustrated it didn't. Maybe he should open his eyes and see that Fate might've been trying to teach *him* a lesson.

Gage and Braden exchanged a look, and based on Gage's sly smile, I knew they had secretly agreed on some form of punishment for my behavior.

"I'm up," Gage said. He started to throw when Nathan stopped him.

"Your foot is over your marker."

We all looked down at his foot, which was several inches past where his marker indicated it should be. "Nathan, don't be anal," Gage said.

"Fine, if you want to cheat, that's on you."

Gage growled and inched his foot back. He chucked his Frisbee. It careened into a bush off to the right. Nathan laughed.

"You got in my head, Nathan."

"You let me in, sucker."

Gage tromped off to find his Frisbee. When he came out of the bush, leaves all over his shirt, he held up his own tie-dyed Frisbee and an additional bright red one. "I found a lost soul."

"The owner's info should be on the back," Jerom said.

Gage turned it over. "Lookie here. This Frisbee belongs to a Miss Lauren Fletcher."

"A girl who plays disc golf?" Jerom said. "That's hot."

Gage curled his lip. "I don't know. A girl who plays disc golf? She's probably a dog. Some aggressive, burly thing."

The guys laughed, not seeming to realize I was standing right there . . . playing disc golf. Maybe that's how they saw me. Maybe that's how most guys saw me.

Nathan grabbed the disc from Gage and shoved it in his equipment bag. "The least we can do is return her Frisbee."

"Be my guest," Gage said.

It wasn't until close to the end of the course that I knew what Braden and Gage had secretly agreed to earlier. As we passed a muddy pond that tried to pretend it was a scenic lake, Braden grabbed me by my arms and Gage took hold of my feet. I kicked and struggled, but they held tight.

"You see, Jerom," Braden said, "let me teach you the

proper way to throw someone into a body of water."

"I've always wondered if my technique was a little off," he said, rubbing the patch of scruffy hair he had grown out on his chin. "Please share ways I can improve."

"Well, first," Gage piped up, and I managed to get a leg free and kick him in the chest. He gasped, but grabbed my leg again. "You swing them. Like so." I moved from side to side in a big, arching swing.

"Okay, yes, I see."

"We're going to get kicked off the course if you throw her in," Nathan said.

"Yes, listen to Nathan, please," I begged. The cattails that filled the pond loomed in my peripheral vision on every downward swing.

Gage laughed. "Who's going to kick us out? The park police?"

"Then," Braden continued, "right when your subject reaches the height of the swing, you let go." And they did just that. I landed with a smack in the shallow water, crushing cattails beneath me. A couple of ducks took flight and I let myself sink into the muddy water that the summer sun had turned into a warm swamp. It oozed between my fingers as I pushed myself off the bottom.

"You two are excellent teachers," Jerom said. "Thank you for imparting your knowledge to me."

I stood, large globs of mud splatting back to their home. "Who needs a spa treatment when I have disc golf mud therapy?" I ran a hand from my shoulder to my wrist, scraping off more mud, and then did the same on the other arm. When I exited I went straight for Gage, ready to give him a big hug. He knew that game and took off running. In my pursuit of Gage, I managed to catch Braden off guard by doubling back. I wrapped my arms around him from behind. "Whose car did we drive today?" I said, my cheek pressed against his back. "Oh, that's right. I call shotgun." I felt him groan.

"Your trunk is pretty big," Nathan spoke up.

I gasped and let go of Braden. "Nathan!"

His cheeks colored. "I wasn't serious."

I smiled. As if he needed to clarify that. Gage came slinking back, keeping a good distance between us.

The players on the course behind us laughed as they took in the scene, then asked, "Uh, can we play through?"

"Yes," I said, water still squishing between my toes as I walked. "Feel free. We're leaving."

"Leaving?" Braden said, faking incredulity. "But we only have two holes left. Come on, Charlie, we can't stop now."

I knew he was making fun of me and what I had done to Dave a few weeks ago in football, when he got the call about his grandma. The veiled rebuke stung. "Okay, let's keep playing."

"I was just kidding." He put his arm around my shoulder.

I shrugged it off. "No, I want to play. You're right, we're almost done."

"But you have mud dropping out of your shorts," Braden said. "And the image isn't a good one."

"Shut up. Who's up?" I asked as the players now ahead of us finished the hole. I picked up a Frisbee and marched to the throwing point.

At the car when we were finished, Braden opened the trunk.

"Don't be a jerk," I said. "I'm not getting in there."

He shot me angry eyes and pulled out a blanket. "I was just getting something for you to sit on." He handed me the blanket.

"Oh. Thanks." I took it and wrapped it around my entire backside. "Sorry." I shouldn't have called him a jerk, even playfully. I knew that word bugged him.

The guys piled into the car, but Jerom stopped me, nodding his head toward where Braden sat in the driver's seat. "How hard is it to let a guy feel useful every once in a while?"

"What?"

"Would it have killed you to listen to his pointers back there?"

I looked at Braden, then back to Jerom. Why would Braden need to feel useful? Had something made him feel un-useful? Was something going on with him that he'd talked to Jerom, the "really good listener," about? A surge of jealousy that Jerom might know something about Braden that I didn't coursed through me. "Yes. It might've killed me."

He rolled his eyes and headed for the passenger seat.

CHAPTER 12

• • • • • • •

When I got to work the next Tuesday, Linda's face was beaming with a smile of giddy anticipation.

"What's up?" I asked.

"Go change and I'll tell you when you get done."

She probably thought it was weird that I brought my work clothes in my backpack and came in wearing my sloppy T-shirts. But I still cared more about what my brothers thought than what she did. And I didn't live in my mind . . . or whatever she had said. I lived in a house full of guys who loved to make fun of me. I walked out after changing and looked at her expectantly.

"Okay, close your eyes," she said.

Playing along, I closed my eyes.

"Ready? Open them."

I did, and she held up a check for a hundred and fifteen dollars. It was made out to me. "What's this?"

"Your cut of the makeup session we did the other day."

I took the check and stared at the number. And here I thought I was going to tell Linda I didn't want to do it anymore. But if I could make over a hundred bucks just sitting there, I could handle it. It meant I'd be able to pay off my dad quicker.

"We did so well, we're going to hold at least two more classes and see how it goes." She pulled a flyer out from under the cupboard and handed it to me. On the upper right-hand corner of the flyer was a picture of me in full makeup.

"Whoa. What's that?"

"Your picture. I thought you were okay with it. It's the one we took the other day."

"I just thought you printed off a few for my . . . family . . ." I would not mention my mom again. It really was eating me up. ". . . to see."

"Did she like them?"

"Yeah. They were great." That wasn't a lie, right?

"I apologize. I should've asked you. It just turned out so well, I offered it to Amber."

I stared at the picture again. It was just a dumb flyer. Hopefully no one would recognize me. My friends and brothers weren't exactly in the market for makeup.

That night I couldn't sleep. My brain kept spinning. It was only midnight, earlier than my normal middle-of-the-night waking, so when I looked out the window and saw the light on in Braden's room, I texted: *Up?*

Yeah, see you in one minute, he texted back almost immediately.

I heard his back door shut right after mine. We arrived at the fence together. He leaned his shoulder against the board and I could smell his deodorant. It was a sharp, clean scent.

"What's up?" he asked.

"Feeling restless." I sat down, back to the fence, and listened as he did the same.

"No run again today?"

"No."

"Are you out here every night you don't run?"

"No. Aside from the two nights with you, I've only been out here one other time."

"You should've texted me."

"It was two in the morning."

"So?"

"I may be selfish, but even I felt bad about that."

He laughed.

I didn't know why I texted him to come out here. It wasn't like I had anything important to discuss. In a way it was nice to know I wasn't alone in my middle-of-the-night world. My brothers slept like the dead. How was it that my brain wouldn't shut off? I felt guilty asking my brothers about my mom. I didn't want to be the one to make everyone else miserable when they had moved on. Maybe they'd moved on because they had real memories to hang on to while my brain had to make up its own. Why did my brain have to be so morbid about it?

"Why do you run so much, anyway?"

"I need to stay in shape for basketball or I'm in pain those first several weeks of practice."

"So you run, what, six . . . seven miles a day to save yourself from two weeks of pain? It seems like you're training for a marathon, not a basketball game."

"Well, it helps me sleep, too."

"Most people don't need to exhaust themselves in order to sleep."

"True. A lot of people just take sleeping pills."

He let out a single laugh, the way he always did when something someone said surprised him. "Yes. I guess your way is more natural." There was a long pause. "You're good at avoiding questions, but what I'm asking is why you can't sleep."

He was just a disembodied voice, I told myself. I could talk to a disembodied voice. Or the moon. I could always talk to the moon. I found it in the sky, minding its own business, only half lit.

Finally, I said, "I have nightmares." He must've sensed it was better to talk as little as possible, because he just waited. "About my mom and the night she died. My brain seems to think it's fun to give me every scenario, even impossible ones. It's pretty much the only memory I have from when I was little . . . that night. I don't even know if any of it is real or if my mind has made all of it up." I had never told anyone about my nightmares, not even Gage, who knew more than most about the inner workings of my brain. It felt strangely freeing, like I was putting it out there for the moon to deal with.

"What happens in them?"

"Different things—rain and breaking windows and cars. And my mom, of course."

"I'm sorry."

"I hate it. Running equals dreamless nights."

"Well, that makes a lot more sense than the basketball excuse."

"It helps for basketball too."

"I'm sure." After several minutes he said, "You learned how to ride your bike when you were four. I was so jealous because I still had training wheels."

I was relieved he had switched to our useless-facts game and said, "I remember your training wheels."

"You do? Because right after you learned how to ride your bike, I spent that entire Saturday learning how to ride without them. You shamed me into it."

I smiled and tried to think of something I remembered about him as a child, to match his fact. "How about in the first grade when you told your teacher that my dad was really your dad and you yelled 'This man is trying to kidnap me' when your father tried to take you home? Your dad was so embarrassed."

"Yes, that was back in the days when I was jealous you all had each other and I didn't have any siblings."

"Now you're trapped in the craziness. You're one of us, baby, whether you want to be or . . ." I trailed off as his real intention of bringing up my bike-riding hit me. He wasn't jumping back into the game. "Wait. I was four?"

"Yes."

"So my mom was alive when I learned how to ride my bike." I searched my memory, trying hard to picture her there, out in front of the house, watching me learn. I could clearly picture my dad holding on to the back of my bike, running along beside me. I kept telling him to let go. He wouldn't. Was my mom watching us?

I squeezed my eyes shut. "Just let me ride around the

block," I had said. "I'll go with her," Jerom offered. He had been riding circles around me. He must've been almost nine at the time. We went around the block, and it wasn't until the first corner that I realized I hadn't practiced turning without training wheels yet. Fear stopped me from trying and I ran straight into the street sign. Jerom picked me up, put me back on the bike, and pointed me in the right direction. I crashed on every single corner, but made it home with only one scraped knee.

Had my mom taken care of it?

No. It was my dad. I knew that. I remembered sitting on the counter as he blew on it and told me I was tough. How was it possible I could have these detailed memories and not remember different times, different events, where my mom spent time with me?

"She looked a lot like you do now."

My throat constricted a little. "Yeah." I already knew that. Aside from the wedding picture in the hall, we had a box of pictures of her. That's how I remembered her, in still snapshots—standing next to me when I blew out three candles on a cake, looking up in surprise from where she sat on the couch reading a book, wearing a baseball cap and cheering on Jerom at his Little League game. I remembered the pictures, not the events. "What else do you remember about her?"

"She was quiet. . . ." He hesitated. "She used to come over and talk to my mom. One time I went into the kitchen where they were talking and she was crying."

"What?"

"I remember it clearly because I was afraid my mom would get mad at me for interrupting them."

"What would my mom have to be sad about?"

"I'm not sure. My mom was rubbing her back and she was—"

"How old were you?" I adjusted my back against the fence.

"I don't know. Around seven, I guess."

"How could you remember that?"

"It's just one of those vivid memories."

Irrational anger surged in my chest and I wasn't sure why. "Well, maybe she was worried about your mom. Maybe she was pleading with your mom to leave your jerk of a dad."

"My dad didn't start drinking until his back injury five years ago." His voice was tight, hurt.

I stood. "Well, my mom had a perfect life, so I don't know what she'd have to be sad about."

"Charlie."

"I'm tired." I went back in the house, letting the door shut harder than I should've.

CHAPTER 13

• • • • • • •

The next morning I woke up to find Gage looking through the makeup catalog Amber had given me. "Is there something you need to tell me?" he asked. "Since when do you . . ."

I threw my pillow at his head. "Maybe I decided to go girly."

"As if. Dad would freak if he saw you in this much makeup. Plus, it's not you."

I didn't understand what that meant. I stared at the girl on the front of the catalog he held. She was soft and feminine and beautiful—like the wedding picture of my mom in the hall. So which part of that wasn't me?

I turned onto my stomach and put my arms over my head. Who was I kidding? None of that was me. "Someone just brought it by my work the other day."

"Amber?" he asked, turning the catalog toward me and showing me her picture in the front where she had circled her name in blue ink. "Is that this girl here? Because if so, you have to introduce us. She's hot."

I rolled out of bed and snatched the catalog from him. "What do you want?"

"We're playing soccer on the beach. Let's go."

"I don't feel like it today."

He stopped cold, then looked around like he was in some alternate world. "Um . . . what? You don't feel like playing soccer?" He put his hand on my forehead, then turned me in a full circle. "What have you done with my sister?"

Truth was, I didn't feel like seeing Braden because I knew I'd behaved badly the night before. What he said had caught me off guard, and I ended up throwing him and his family under a bus to make myself feel better. And even though I knew it hurt him, what he had said still bothered me, so I wasn't quite ready to apologize.

"I have to work in a few hours." I didn't have to work today at all. He didn't notice my lie.

"That whole work thing is really cramping your style. You need to talk to Dad about the fact that you've learned your lesson. I'm sure he just wanted to see if you'd get a job."

"Yeah, I'm sure. I'll talk to him soon." Later. I was finally making good money . . . and work wasn't as bad as it had seemed at first. It was something different that my brothers had never done, and I kind of liked that.

"So really? No soccer?"

"Really."

As I was folding shirts on tables at work the next day, Linda began folding next to me. "Your aura is blue today. Most of the time that means sadness. Is everything okay?"

Wow, even my aura was upset about my tiff with Braden. "I'm fine." I folded another shirt. "It's just weird when a belief you've had your whole life is suddenly challenged."

"What belief is that?"

"Nothing. I just pictured someone a certain way, and maybe they weren't that way at all." Maybe I had no memories of my mom because she was never around.

"That's hard, when someone doesn't meet our expectations." She moved around to the other side of the table. "Sometimes we expect more than people are capable of giving at that moment."

Shouldn't a mother be capable of being there for her kids? Was that too much to expect?

She was there. It was my memories that weren't.

"Honey." Linda touched my hand. I wasn't used to such a soft touch. It made my stomach feel hollow. I moved my hand to the next shirt to break the contact. "If you need to go home, I understand."

"No. No, I don't. I'm totally fine." And I was. I didn't need to get caught up in the stupid emotion of this. I could shake it off.

"Do you want to talk about it? Tell me more about this person?"

"No."

She paused as if expecting me to change my mind. I wasn't going to change my mind.

"Okay. I'm going to crunch some numbers in the back."

"Sounds good."

I continued folding shirts. A movement by the window caught my eye, and I looked up in time to see a mother and daughter walk by arm in arm. The two of them walking together made me think of how it could've been now if my mom were still here. We would've spent time together—talked, laughed, shared stories only she would understand, shared secrets I couldn't tell anyone else. The pit in my stomach seemed to expand with that feeling. I didn't like it. Why was I suddenly feeling like something was missing in my life?

I had a great life. Linda and her concerned looks and gentle touch didn't need to come around and make me think my life wasn't amazing. *I'll run eight miles in the morning.* That would take care of this.

CHAPTER 14

• • • • • • •

I walked into the kitchen to get a water bottle for my run and found Nathan staring intently at the red Frisbee on the counter.

"What's wrong?" I asked.

"I can't do it. I can't call her."

"You're returning her Frisbee, Nathan, not asking her out. Just dial the number."

"You're right. I know you're right."

I opened the fridge and grabbed a water bottle. When I turned around, Nathan was in the exact same position.

"If you were Lauren and some guy called you to return your Frisbee, what would you think?" he asked.

I pulled my foot to my butt to stretch out my thigh. "I'd think that some guy was calling me to return my Frisbee."

He grunted. "Yeah, but you're not a normal girl, so that doesn't count."

The ache in my stomach twitched, and I cringed.

"Normal girls read into everything."

Switching feet, I stretched the other leg. "And what exactly are you doing right now?"

"I'm not reading into anything, I'm psyching myself out."

I grabbed the phone off the counter and dialed Lauren's number. "There. It's done." I thrust the phone toward him.

He held up his hands and wouldn't take it from me, jumping away from it like it was an opposing team's mascot or something.

"Ugh. You're such a wimp." I put it up to my ear.

"Hello?" a girl answered.

"Hi. Is this Lauren?"

"Yes." She sounded like a completely normal girl—whatever that meant.

"My brothers and I were playing disc golf out at Woodward Park the other day and found one of your Frisbees."

"Oh. Awesome. I guess putting the info on the back really works."

"Yeah. So what do you want me to do with it?" Disc golf Frisbees weren't like standard cheapie plastic things. They were weighted and high-quality, so I knew she'd want it back. I happened to glance up at Nathan, and he was clutching the Frisbee in two hands, staring at me.

"Can I come get it, maybe?" Lauren asked. "Do you live near Woodward?"

"Not really. We're actually about five minutes east of the mall, by Hillman Park."

"Oh, cool, that's not too far from me. Will you text me your address?"

"Yes, but I'm getting ready to leave. My brother Nathan will be here, though." And he owed me big for this.

"Okay. Thanks."

I hung up, then texted her our address.

"Did she sound cute?" he asked.

"Nope, she sounded like a big, burly girl. Have fun."

I lay on my bed, throwing a soccer ball in the air over and over. It was midnight. I couldn't face sleep. I wondered if Gage, whose room shared a wall with mine, was going to come over and tell me to be quiet. I caught the ball with a loud smack and then pulled my arm back, poised to hurl it against the wall this time. That would wake him.

I sighed and let it roll off my fingertips instead, landing on the floor with a thud. I didn't want to talk to Gage. I wanted to talk to Braden. I needed to apologize. That's why my bedroom light was still on, after all—a hope that he would see it. His room was dark, though. I sat up and planted my feet on the ground. Forcing myself to stand up, I walked to the light switch and flipped it off, then lay back down again.

The curtains on my bedroom window weren't drawn tightly closed, and a strip of light from the moon cut across my ceiling. It was as if the moon were trying to tell me to stop being so stubborn. I stood again and marched down the stairs and outside. Then I sat there in the dirt by the fence. I should've just texted him, but I couldn't. What if he ignored it? At least this way if he didn't come, I could tell myself it was because he was asleep.

I wasn't sure how much time passed as I sat there. Long enough for me to wonder why I was still sitting there. I stood and paced the fence. If he didn't come out by the time I counted to fifty, I'd go back inside and forget about this. I started my count. When I reached forty-nine, I decided that one hundred was a much better number. I needed to give him a chance, after all. Fifty seconds was barely more time than a center got to snap a football.

The numbers ticked through my head, one for each

step I took along the fence line. "Seventy-six," I whispered aloud, my bare foot landing on a rock. "Ouch." I stopped and clenched my fists. This was ridiculous. Just as I turned to head back to the house, I heard his back door snick shut. I whirled to face the fence again and watched him walk slowly toward it. He didn't know I was there. I should call out to him. If he did know I was there, would he tell me how heartless I was for what I said the other night?

I was surprised when he walked right up to my board and leaned his forehead against it. "Hey," he said.

I leaned into the board as well. "Hi," I whispered. "I didn't think you could see me."

"You're wearing white. It practically glows through the cracks."

I looked down at my basketball camp T-shirt. "Oh."

"Are you still mad at me?" he asked.

"No . . ." I closed my eyes and took a deep breath. Relief flooded my body. I had missed him more than I realized. "I'm sorry."

"For what?"

"For what I said about your mom and dad. My family is far from perfect—you know that as well as anyone. I'm sorry for turning it around on you. I was just surprised." I shoved my hands into the pockets of my sweats. "Maybe my mom was different than I imagined her."

"Your family is pretty amazing, Charles." I heard him draw in a deep breath. Maybe he was relieved we were talking again too. "I shouldn't have said that about your mom. I wasn't thinking. Here you were upset you couldn't remember anything about her and what do I do? Give you these depressing memories that aren't even yours. There were so many reasons she could've been sad. Maybe your brothers were fighting too much that day and she was at her wit's end. She had four kids in six years. That had to get overwhelming at times."

Unlike when we sat back-to-back against the fence, I could feel his breath seep through the crack and touch my cheeks. I still didn't open my eyes. We were so close that the air smelled like him. I didn't realize I knew how Braden smelled until that moment. "Thank you." I twisted, turning away from his scent, which was making my head spin. I put my back to the fence once again, then looked up at the night stars.

He didn't do the same thing, because his voice was crystal clear next to my ear. "My dad *is* a jerk and my mom should leave him."

"No. I shouldn't have said that. He's sick. If he would just stop drinking—"

"It didn't start five years ago. I mean, the drinking did, but he was always a jerk. You know that. The alcohol just makes it worse. Why do you think I claimed your dad was mine at school that day? I wanted him to be mine. I wanted to be in your family."

"You are in our family."

"No, I'm not."

"In all the ways that matter. I told you the other night that you're stuck. You can't disown us now."

"I don't want to," he whispered. My heart thought that was the time to beat out of control. I tried to respond, but I couldn't think of anything to say. The fence between us had never felt like a barrier to me. It had always felt like protection—the only reason I was able to say some of the things I could out here. But tonight, I wanted to feel him next to me. I wanted to comfort him.

He took two deep breaths, then said, "You missed one of the funniest tantrums ever on the field the other day over a supposed foul."

I relaxed, glad he changed the subject. My reaction had proved it was getting too intense. "George?"

"Of course."

"Who fouled him?"

"That's the point. Nobody fouled him."

"So you did, then. What did you do?"

He laughed. "I barely tripped him. Barely! He didn't even fall. I was going for the ball. His foot just got in the way. Nobody else would've called it."

"George is a baby."

"Yes. Never date anyone you haven't seen play sports. It says so much about a guy."

It was true that you could tell a lot about someone by the way they played a game. I knew Jerom was a leader, Nathan followed all the rules to a T, and Gage was laidback, in it for the fun. What about Braden? What had I learned about Braden over the years from watching him play? He was a team player, never hogged the ball or took it when he couldn't deliver. He hung in the background a lot, waiting until someone needed assistance. So he was . . . what? Observant? Not selfish?

"And never, ever date a guy who acts like he's playing in the finals of a professional sporting event when he's really playing a pickup game."

We had laughed about that a lot. People who took a pickup game so seriously that they lost their temper or threw a tantrum over the stupidest things. "What if he *is* playing in the finals of a professional sporting event?"

"Then it's perfectly acceptable. And you should find out about getting free season tickets."

I laughed. "Which brings me back to the fact game. I have one. If you could only have season tickets to one sport it would be baseball. A's."

"Are you sure? There are so many sports I like. This could be the fact that you lose over."

"Only if I get it wrong and you can answer the same

fact about me and get it right. But I'm not worried. You leave puddles of drool on the floor when you watch the A's play. If you could watch even one game in the Coliseum, I think your heart would stop."

He let out a short burst of air. "Yes. It's true. But I don't think I know this answer about you."

"I've known all along that I know you better. It just took me a while to prove it."

"Can we institute a three-strike rule?"

"Nope."

"Fine. Give me a minute to ponder it, then."

I hummed the *Jeopardy!* theme song. The funny thing was that I didn't know if *I* knew the answer to this question about myself. I would love watching almost any sport live. So technically, I'd probably let him get away with any answer as long as it was a team I really liked.

"Your brother." He said it with so much confidence that I almost immediately believed him. But then I realized what he said made no sense.

"What?"

"If you could have season tickets to any sporting event, it would be the UNLV Rebels soccer team so you could watch every one of your brother's games from the stands. You would be in heaven."

I started to deny it, to say that wasn't technically a match because it wasn't a professional team, but then I remembered how sad I felt every time Jerom told me he had played in a game and I wasn't there.

"You should see the look on your face when you watch your brothers play. I don't think I've ever seen anyone more proud than you."

I couldn't say anything. I didn't trust my voice. He was right. There were no other games in the world I'd rather watch than ones involving my brothers.

"I know it's not technically season tickets or a professional sports team, but I think it's the most accurate."

He was right. He did know me well. Better than I thought he would. I didn't think he'd been paying such close attention over the years. He was always around, and being a year younger I was always interested in what he and my brother were doing. But I didn't think it went both ways. "Yeah, it counts," I said quickly.

"What was that?"

"Yes."

"Your voice sounds funny."

"Yeah, well, your face looks funny. See you tomorrow." I walked away from his laughter.

"Who knows who better now?" he called out.

I shook my head with a smile. He was pretty good. I'd have to step up my facts. He would not beat me at this game.

CHAPTER 15

● ● ● ● ● ● ●

I wiped my feet on the mat and opened the back door. The kitchen was dimly lit by the light above the stove. I shut the door slowly, locked it, then turned around. Gage sat on the counter with a bowl of cereal. I jumped, catching the scream in my throat before it came out.

"You scared me."

He looked at the door behind me, then back to me. "What are you doing and why did you have a goofy grin on your face when you came in here? You sneaking around? Is there some boy I need to beat up?"

My cheeks flushed involuntarily. Nobody knew about

my fence chats with Braden, and I planned to keep it that way. "No. I'm not sneaking around. I was walking around the yard because you wouldn't run with me tonight and I couldn't sleep." Before he had a chance to analyze that statement I turned it on him. "Did you just get home? Dad is going to kill you."

"No. I've been home. I just got hungry."

I pulled a bowl from the cupboard and poured myself some Cocoa Krispies. He slid over a little and I joined him on the counter.

"Are you saying you'd tattle on me if I'd just gotten home?"

I took a bite of cereal and nodded. "Yes. I'm tired of being the one in trouble. Maybe he'd make you get a job."

Gage flashed me his smile. "Ooh. You think Linda would hire me? I could help girls pick out clothes. I'd be good at that."

"Flirting with girls is not the same as helping them, Gage."

He shrugged. "Dad would never make me get a job anyway. I'm his favorite."

"We all know Nathan is his favorite."

"True. Well, I'm positive I was Mom's favorite."

My spoon stopped halfway to my mouth and my eyes darted to his. It wasn't often the word *Mom* was used in our house. Gage was only a year older than me. I thought there was no way he could remember any more than I did.

"Were you?" I asked in a voice just above a whisper.

He tousled my hair and slid off the counter. "It was just a joke, Charlie. I'm sure Mom didn't have a favorite." He placed his empty bowl in the sink. "But if she did, it was me. Who could resist this face?"

"Me, for one."

"Oh, please. You are the most easily persuaded. You do anything I ask."

I kicked him in the side and he let out a grunt. "In your dreams."

"No kicking."

I kicked him again, but this time he grabbed my foot. "Seriously, that hurts. If you didn't have massive legs, I'd let you kick me."

"Massive?"

"Have you seen your thigh muscles lately? Your soccer coach is going to be so happy."

I yanked my foot away from him, sloshing milk onto my hand. I wiped the milk on my sweats and took another bite. "Did she ever go to any of your games?"

"What? Who?"

I could barely swallow my mouthful of cereal. "Mom. Did she ever go to any of your soccer games?"

"You think I remember? I was seven when . . ." He trailed off. It's not like he needed to finish. I knew. We all knew how that sentence ended. *When she died.* When her car slid off the road in the rain and into a ditch. And normally that sentence tightened across my chest and wouldn't let go for several minutes. But today, my brain clung to the first part of his statement. He didn't remember. Just like me. So we were just too young to have any real memories. Or . . . or nothing. We were too young.

"I'm going to bed," he said.

I nodded, kind of regretting pushing the Mom topic. This was why I didn't do it. It had a way of turning even Gage sad. I wished I hadn't gotten a bowl of cereal because now I felt like I had to finish it. And instead of the giddy feelings I'd brought inside after my talk with Braden, my stomach hurt. Gage paused, took a breath like he was going to say something, then stopped. I held my breath in anticipation, but then his eyes drifted to the back door. I worried he was going to put two and two together about Braden and me. So I did the only thing I could think of. I flung a spoonful of Cocoa Krispies at him.

Saturday morning arrived, much to my stomach's dismay. It bombarded me with nervous flutters the likes of which I hadn't known since trying out for the basketball team my freshman year. I knew I couldn't get out of lunch with Amber and her friends today. But if I went they would find out I was a fraud. That I knew nothing about anything they'd want to talk about. Girls like her didn't give me the time of day at school. Granted, I'd surrounded myself well, with my wall of brothers on one side and my teammates on the other, but girls like Amber didn't really mix with girls like me. We had nothing in common. I wasn't looking forward to it. I pulled some of my "cute" clothes out of the back of my closet and threw them in my backpack to change into at work.

"Charlie, can I talk to you?" my dad called from the kitchen as I headed for the front door.

"Sure." I wheeled back around and poked my head through the kitchen doorway. For a second, panic rushed through me, thinking Gage had told my dad about me roaming the yard at one a.m. But then I remembered this was Gage. He wouldn't tell on me.

"You've been working hard," my dad said, gesturing toward the bar stool in front of him.

I sat down. "Yeah, I guess."

"I think we've both proved the point. I know you have basketball camp starting soon."

I nodded. Four weeks. And I'd been wondering if it was going to be a fight to let me go.

"Have you earned enough to pay off your most recent ticket?"

"Yes."

"Then why don't you take it easy until camp starts?"

"I don't have to work anymore?"

"No."

I smiled, excited that I could have my summer back, but then Linda's face flashed through my mind and I felt guilty. "I can't just quit like that. I should probably give my boss a couple weeks' notice."

"That would be very responsible of you."

I didn't want to be responsible. I wanted to quit. Before I had to go out today with the girls I had nothing in common with. "Okay. Thanks, Dad. Um . . . I'll be home a little later today."

"You have a longer shift?"

"No . . . I'm going out with a coworker after . . . if that's okay."

"Do I know him?"

"Oh, it's a girl. Me and a couple of girls are going to hang out."

My father gave me the most bewildered look in the world, not helping my confidence at all. "And do what?"

"Whatever girls do."

He laughed. "You have no idea what that is, do you?"

"Sure I do . . . sort of."

"Well, try to at least look like you're having fun."

"Thanks." I slid off the stool.

"What's in the bag?" My dad pointed to the backpack I held at my side.

"Um . . . just . . . girl stuff. You know."

He lowered his brow for a moment, then his eyes went wide. "Oh. Right. You got that covered? Everything good?"

I tried not to laugh. "Yep. All good." My dad, trying to explain my period to me on that fateful day four years ago, was an experience I'll never forget. He sounded like a science book. He fumbled through the technicalities, then bought me some pads and left me to myself. I had to read the instructions.

I exited the kitchen and crossed the living room. On my way out the front door, I slammed into Braden, who was coming in.

"Shoot," I gasped, flying backward.

He grabbed hold of my arms, preventing me from falling. Something he would've never done pre–fence chat. He would've let me fall on my butt and then I would've tried to sweep his legs out from beneath him. Our eyes met for the briefest of moments and then he quickly released me. As if realizing he'd breached some unwritten rule, he grabbed my arm, bent down, and threw me over his shoulder.

Walking to the couch, he unceremoniously plopped me down on my back. "There. If you're going to fall on your *butt*," he said, his eyes twinkling as he said the word, "choose a better place."

Instinct taking over, my hand shot out and grabbed him by the wrist before he could walk away. This is where I would've placed a foot to his ribs or a head to his stomach and then felt like I had won. Instead, instinct didn't follow through and I froze, lying on my back on the couch, holding his wrist. It was strong and familiar. His skin was lighter than mine, and I studied the way my fingers looked against his skin. *Disengage,* my brain yelled, *this is Braden, Gage's best friend,* but my hand wouldn't open.

A flicker of confusion passed across his face, then a softening of his brow, almost like he wanted to lean closer. But then he tightened his jaw and dropped an elbow down on my stomach. It wasn't hard, but unexpected, so it knocked the wind out of me. I took a gasping breath of air, relief flooding through me.

"I think that's two to zip, sistah," he said, inches from my face, then stood up and walked away.

What was wrong with me? I silently thanked him for calling me his *sistah.* It reminded me of our history. Our years of history. I clenched and unclenched my hand. It felt hot. Every inch of me felt hot. I needed to stop the way my body was reacting to Braden lately. We were friends. Too close to ever want to explore these stupid new reactions and risk losing him forever. I stood and practically ran out of the house.

If I thought the previous week of makeup was bad, this week was nothing short of torturous. Two hours! I kept track this time. How could a person spend two hours working on my face? Granted, there were a lot of questions and much more makeup. I could see my eyelashes when I blinked. It was weird. But two hours? I could've played an entire basketball game in that time, with time-outs, halftime, foul shots, and everything.

Her friends from last week met us after the session was over.

"I'm going to wash my face," I said, pointing toward the back. Maybe they would forget about me and leave while I was gone.

"No way. We are going out as the beauty queens we are," Amber said, grabbing my arm. "You look amazing. Don't touch my work of art."

Or not.

CHAPTER 16

• • • • • • •

We sat in the corner booth of a café, drinking iced drinks and talking. Well, Amber the Olympic talker was doing most of the talking, but I was surprisingly entertained. And not just because a Cubs game was playing on the television mounted in the corner. We talked about the last books we'd read and the subjects at school we struggled in (math for me). I was actually able to contribute to those conversations. So maybe they weren't much different from my teammates and me. Then we moved on to boys.

"I swear all they think about is food and sex," Savannah said.

I laughed. "No. That's not true. I have three brothers. They actually do have other thoughts."

"Like what?"

"Like everything. My brother Nathan took ten minutes to call a girl the other day."

"Why?"

"Because he was overanalyzing it and was insecure. And my brother Gage uses humor to cover how he really feels. And Jerom, he worries about everything."

Amber smiled. "Awesome. Charlie gets to be the Guy Interpreter now."

"Yeah, I'm not sure I'm ready for a title or anything."

"And speaking of guys that need interpreting, I can no longer ignore that table," Amber said.

"I know," Savannah said, "they are totally staring."

"I thought we were just pretending they didn't exist," Antonia added.

"Who? What?" I asked.

They laughed. "Those guys," Amber said.

"Okay, they realized we noticed them," Savannah said. "I give them two minutes before they walk over here."

"Two minutes is kind of generous," Antonia said.

I still hadn't looked. What if they were friends with my brothers?

"See, I told you," Antonia said.

This time I looked and saw a guy walking our way. He grabbed a chair by the back on his way and slid it across the tile floor until it rested right in front of our table. Then he sat down. I didn't know him. This made me happy.

"Can I help you?" Amber said, cool and professional.

"We wondered if you ladies wanted to join us."

"Sorry, girl time," Amber said. "Which obviously means girls only."

I wondered if Amber and the others had guys hit on them like this all the time. It was a first for me to be on the receiving end of this exchange, and I found it amusing. I held back a laugh and waited to hear what line he'd deliver. I could probably give him some pointers. My brothers were experts. Right now he was playing the Gage of our group. Gage could never hold himself back. He had to jump in with both feet, even though Jerom and Braden would tell him to play it cool for a while.

I wondered who this guy was interested in. Probably Amber. She was the prettiest, with the typical Barbie-doll look—blond hair, blue eyes, perfect teeth, tan. Or maybe Antonia; she had the most beautiful shade of mocha skin.

He folded his arms across his chest. "Oh, I see how it is. You should've hung up a sign that said 'No boys allowed.'"

I gave a little laugh. He shouldn't have pulled out the injured-ego play so early. It was not endearing. What he should've done was said something like, *I can hold my own in a girls' club, try me.* Maybe my title should've been Moderator instead of Interpreter. I decided to help him out because it was obvious he needed it. And he was pretty cute, just a little clueless.

"I bet he'd fit right in with the girls' club," I said, and everyone looked at me.

"For sure," he said, a smile lighting up his face.

"Let's test him. Four questions every girl would know. We each get one. If you answer right, you get half an hour."

Amber smiled, seeming to like this game.

"I'll start," I said. "Name four makeup items."

The girls scoffed. "Too easy."

"For a girl," he said. I agreed. I didn't think my brothers could name two.

He looked up, biting his lip. "Okay, um, that black stuff you put on your eyelashes."

"Official names," I said.

"Wait, I'm thinking." He slapped the table. "Mascara?"

"Good."

"Then there's"—he pointed to his lips—"lipstick."

"That's two."

"Cheek color."

Amber laughed. "Is that your final answer?"

"No. It's . . ." The other guys wandered over. "Cheek stuff, guys," he said. "What's it called?"

"No help from your friends," Antonia said.

"Maybe we should let them put their brains together," I said. Especially since one of the guys who walked over was hot and I wouldn't mind him hanging out for a while. They huddled for a minute, whispering, and Amber giggled. "This is fun," she said. I checked out the score on the TV while the guys were busy.

"Okay, we have an answer," he announced. "Blush."

"Very good. That's three. One more."

"Did you already do mascara?" Hot Guy asked.

"Yeah, and lipstick."

"*Is* there anything else?" the other guy, a redhead, asked.

"So much more," Amber assured them.

The original guy snapped his fingers. "Oh, oh, what about that brown stuff they use to cover their zits and stuff."

Antonia gasped and I laughed. "What's it called?"

"No idea."

Hot Guy studied me for a minute and I shifted uncomfortably in my seat. "What's the stuff on their eyelids?" he asked. I had almost forgotten I had stuff on my eyelids. Stuff all over my face.

"Shadow something . . . eye shadow!" the first guy yelled. "Passed."

"You still have three more questions, and that was the easy one," Amber said.

"Bring it."

The redhead grabbed another chair. There were three of them and four of us. How did that work, I wondered, when we were odd-numbered like that? Hot Guy hovered by my side of the booth, and since I sat on the end, I scooted over and offered him the seat next to me. He took it. He smelled really good, like cherry ChapStick and something clean . . . laundry detergent, maybe.

"My turn," Amber said. "Name two updo hairstyles."

"Updo?" the first guy asked.

"Yes, hairstyles where your hair is up instead of down."

"Ponytail," Redhead said.

"Okay, I'll count that. One more."

"What's that twisty one called?" the first guy asked.

They all shrugged. I had no idea what it was called either. It was sad that I was following their thought processes more than the girls', who were laughing smugly.

"What about the librarian ball thingy?"

"A bun. It's totally a bun. Next question."

Antonia was quick with her question, as though she'd thought of it the minute she heard the game. "What is the sheer second skin we wear on our legs like pants?"

"Nylons," Redhead answered without a second thought.

The other two looked at him and groaned.

"What?" he said. "I was in a play."

"Then you should know all these answers."

"Whatever."

"Okay, last question," the first guy said, looking at Savannah. She pursed her lips together as though trying to think of something they would never guess. Then her eyes lit up. "Who wrote *Pride and Prejudice*?"

Everyone went instantly silent.

"A little help here," the guy next to me said under his breath.

"Absolutely no idea," I said.

"Shouldn't all the girls in the group be able to answer the question as well?" he said aloud, calling me out.

"I assure you every girl will know the answer to that."

I tried to give Amber wide eyes, telling her not to make any such assurances.

"Then if all of you can't, we win by default?" he asked.

"You are such a punk," I said, and he smiled, his eyes lighting up.

"Yeah, okay," Amber agreed to his addendum.

I raised my hand in shame. "I don't know the answer."

The guys cheered, and Savannah huffed playfully and

threw a wadded-up napkin at me.

"Sorry," I said, holding up my hands to fend off the other napkins that came flying my way.

"So, what do we win?" Hot Guy asked.

"We get to hang out for thirty minutes," the first guy said. "They weren't going to give us the time of day."

Hot Guy met my eyes. "Now we get the time of day?" My heart gave a flip.

"Apparently."

"What does the time of day entail?"

I shrugged.

"Names, definitely names," the first guy said. "And phone numbers," he seemed to add on a whim.

"No way. You earned thirty minutes . . . and names. I'm Amber."

"I'm Dustin," the first guy said. Dustin had floppy blond hair and a smattering of freckles across his nose. He looked like a guy I played softball with a few years back.

"Antonia," she said with a small wave.

"Savannah."

I gave a head nod that I stopped short. "Charlie."

Redhead waved. "I'm Luke and . . ."

He pointed to the guy sitting next to me and was about to say his name when Hot Guy looked straight at me and said, "I'm Evan." Evan had beautiful olive skin and deep brown eyes.

"So where are you ladies coming from?" Dustin asked, and I turned my attention away from Evan and back to him.

"A makeup session," Amber said at the same time I said, "Work." I did not want to tell these guys what we'd been doing. I was embarrassed. If I could've convinced them we had been playing soccer with that much makeup on, I might've.

"We work with makeup," Antonia said, covering for me.

It took a second to realize that these were guys, not my friends. Guys who were trying to pick us up, not ask us if we were interested in a pickup game. They weren't looking to make fun of me.

"That's what I meant," I said. This brought lots of questions about what exactly we did. My eyes kept drifting to the game on the television as the guys asked the stupidest questions ever. The Cubs were down by one and it was the bottom of the ninth. I groaned when Castillo struck out, leaving only one more chance to score. And everybody knew Borbon was not a clutch hitter. Most people in this area were Giants fans, but we were A's all the way, which was why I was voting for the Cubs.

"This is their last chance to score," Evan said, pointing at the screen. "They have two outs."

I almost said "Duh" but bit my tongue. Jerom's voice echoed through my head: *How hard is it to let a guy feel useful every once in a while?* So instead I just nodded, because I couldn't bring myself to say "Please tell me more." But for some reason he must've thought that's exactly what I meant, because he started explaining the game to me in layman's terms, saying things like "The guys in the white shirts really need to put that ball over the fence and then they'll be a shoo-in for the playoffs." I almost said "Actually, they aren't anywhere near making the playoffs this year, but at least it will end their three-game losing streak and let them win back a little dignity and some much-needed confidence." But again, probably not letting him feel useful.

"There, now the coach is telling the pitcher what to throw." The camera had focused in on the coach.

I knew for a fact that Posey, the Giants' catcher, called the games. And even if the manager was calling the pitch, as many did, he'd be giving the signals to the catcher, not the pitcher. It was killing me not to correct him, but my brothers would've been so proud that I didn't. The inside of my mouth tasted a bit salty from my teeth clenching down on my cheeks, though.

"You like to watch baseball?" Evan asked.

"Yeah."

"My dad has four season tickets to the A's. Maybe we could double sometime with one of your friends."

I tried to contain the rush of joy that burst in my chest.

"Yeah, I have a friend who would love you forever if you took us," I said, thinking how Braden would owe me big for this. Then it occurred to me, quite suddenly, that Evan probably meant one of my girl friends sitting at the table, not one of my guy friends.

"Yeah?"

I crossed my arms in front of me, realizing I had gripped the edge of the table in my excitement. "Um. I mean, yes, I can probably find a friend to come."

He grabbed a napkin from the holder. "I guess maybe I should get your number then so I can arrange that."

I told him my number and he wrote it down, then tucked it in his jeans pocket. Amber gave me a head tilt that seemed to say I gave that away too easily. But she was too busy talking to know I'd just scored A's tickets. Sure, I'd have to go with Mr. I Will Impart All My Mediocre Knowledge of Baseball to You, but considering he was hot and nice, that was definitely a sacrifice I was willing to make.

CHAPTER 17

• • • • • •

It was midnight. I didn't think Evan would call at midnight, but I sat at my desk in my room staring at my phone anyway. I should've gotten his number so I didn't have to give up all the control like this. I rubbed my eyes, now makeup-free, and wondered if Evan still would've asked for my number if he could see me now: sweats, tangled hair, tired eyes, and all.

My phone chimed and I gasped.

Are you up? It was Braden.

My arms tingled with goose bumps and I rubbed them. *Yes.* I switched off my lamp, silently accusing myself of leaving it on for Braden in the first place, then made my way outside.

"Where were you all day today?" Braden asked from the other side of the fence.

"I had to work." If I wanted to tell anyone about my makeup sessions, it was Braden—but I didn't want to tell anyone.

"All day?"

"I went out afterward."

"You did?" The surprise in his voice made me realize he thought I meant on a date.

"No, with some girls," I said quickly.

"You did?" He sounded even more surprised.

I laughed. "Yes. And it was weird."

"How so?"

"Well, I thought maybe they wouldn't like me, but they did."

"Why wouldn't they like you?"

"Because I don't know anything about shopping or hair or whatever."

He laughed. "And you think that's all girls like to do?"

"I don't know. Maybe I thought that's what normal girls liked." I didn't have a frame of reference.

"What do you mean by 'normal girls'?"

"Girls that aren't into sports. The only girls I've ever hung out with are a lot like me. Big and burly," I added to lighten the mood that suddenly seemed heavier than I wanted it to.

"You are not big or burly, Charlie. You're tall and strong. There's a big difference. And maybe you're the normal one and those other girls are un-normal."

I laughed at that as I thought of Amber—the pinnacle of every guy's dream. "Whatever. It doesn't bother me. It was just how I felt today. Weird." But not necessarily bad. I actually liked Amber, and maybe that was weird too. "What about you? What did you do today?"

"Watched an NBA classic."

"Ugh. I hate watching those."

"I know."

I smiled. There was something comforting in that moment about Braden knowing me so well. Maybe it was because I'd just hung out with a bunch of people who didn't know me at all. "Really? You know?"

"Yes. You hate them because you already know who wins. But sometimes it's fun to watch a game when the winner is already determined."

"Where's the excitement in that?" I bit my lip, the smile still lingering there. "Was it Jordan?"

"Of course." I thought I heard a smile in his voice. Maybe he was happy I knew him so well too.

"He is amazing to watch. That fade-away jumper."

I put my hand over my heart even though he couldn't see me.

"And those are the kinds of things a normal girl should know," he said.

I laughed. "In your dreams."

"Then I should probably get to those." He stood with a grunt. "Good night, Charlie."

"Did those count as our facts tonight, then?"

"Of course. But if you need another one, you snore in your sleep."

I gasped. "What?"

"Gage's room is right next to yours. I think I'll get you that snoring machine for your birthday."

"Snoring machine?"

"You know, that machine that has a mask and you wear it at night and it stops you from snoring."

I knew he was using his hands to try to describe it and I pressed my lips together to keep from laughing. "I have no idea what you're talking about."

"You know exactly what I'm talking about."

I laughed. I did. "Well, you drool in your sleep."

"Only when I'm really tired."

"I think I'm going to get you a drooling machine. It has this mask thing and these straps . . ."

"Funny."

"I thought so." I stood, brushed off my flannel pajama

bottoms, and walked backward a few steps, my eyes still on the fence.

"Today was boring," he said. "Don't work all day again."

My heart did a flip and I chastised it. He just wanted to play ball or something and had no one around to play with . . . except my brothers and everyone else. "Good night, Braden." I whirled around and jogged to the house, trying to contain my smile.

I stared intently at the shirts lined up on the rack, their colors blending. Why was I having such a hard time telling Linda I had to quit? Maybe because I sort of liked my job. It was relaxing. The last customer told me I was easy to shop around because I was laid-back and no-pressure, but very helpful. I'd never been told something like that before and it felt good.

"Could you re-dress the window mannequin?" Linda asked.

"Sure." I turned around and held out my hand, expecting her to have an outfit for me to dress it in. When she didn't, I was confused. "In what?"

"Why don't you pick something out? She's been wearing the same thing for a couple weeks."

"You don't want me picking something out."

"Sure I do." She pointed to the outfit I wore. I had

layered one of the sheer silky shirts she had me buy over a different-patterned tank top I had picked up on my own. I hadn't been sure if they went together but I thought it looked nice. Was she about to tell me it looked awful? "You'll do a great job."

I sighed, then walked the store. I picked a lacy skirt off the far wall and matched it with a summery-looking shirt. As I undressed the window mannequin, I said, "Linda, every summer I go to basketball camp for a week."

"How fun. I didn't know you played basketball."

"Yes. I do. And camp starts in a few weeks."

"Oh." She pulled out her purse and dug through it, coming up with a little planner. She flipped the pages. "So what are the dates again?"

"August first through the eighth."

She wrote something down. "Sounds good. I marked you down for that week off."

"Oh." Time off. I liked that idea better. "Thank you." I continued to unbutton the mannequin's shirt.

"You may not think you have style, Charlie," Linda said, appraising the clothes I had hung on the hook next to me, "but that clothing combination isn't a basic one. You picked up on the lace theme, not the color scheme. That says a lot."

That compliment shouldn't have made me so proud.

I had probably seen a customer buy this outfit or something.

"Did I tell you that our business is up ten percent since we started stocking the makeup?"

"No, that's great." I folded the removed clothes and slid the shirt I had selected over the neck of the headless lady. Then I stared at the white, unbending arm, wondering how I was supposed to get that into the sleeve.

"It is great." She put her purse back beneath the counter.

"Um . . ." I tried to twist the arm up and it popped off and clanked to the floor.

Linda looked up and laughed when she saw my face. "It pops right back on. You'll get the hang of it. I'll be right back." And with that she disappeared into the back, leaving me with a one-armed mannequin.

I eventually realized the arms had to come off to fit the shirt on, but I had no idea how the skirt would fit over her wide stance. I laid her on her back and kneeled beside her, shimmying the lacy skirt up her legs.

This is how Skye found me when she walked into the store. "Hey, Charlie."

"Hi. Linda's in the back."

We both looked at the half-dressed dummy on the floor then back at each other. Skye laughed.

"Any tips on mannequin dressing?"

"Surprisingly, I've never done it before." She stepped forward and grabbed hold of the legs, trying to shove them together. "Oh. They don't move."

"Yeah."

"Here. I'll hold her neck and you shove her skirt on."

"This feels so wrong," I said as we both took our positions.

"She has no head, so she doesn't know she's being violated."

I laughed and finally got the skirt to her waist. We hoisted her to her feet and both stared at her.

Skye tilted her head. "Are her arms lopsided?" She tried to move the right arm up and it popped off. "I broke her."

"No, it goes back on."

She swung the arm and smacked me on the butt with the mannequin's hand.

"Hey, I have a head and am fully aware when I've been violated."

Skye laughed, and I popped the arm back on and shoved the mannequin into the window before we messed her up even more.

"Thanks for rescuing me."

"No problem." Skye headed for the back and Linda, but stopped. "Oh, remember that band I was telling you about? My boyfriend, Henry's?"

"Yes."

She pulled a flyer out of her purse and pointed to a picture of a flattened toad on the front. "It's this Friday. Right up the street. You should come."

"Yeah. I'll try. Thanks."

"No problem." I watched her walk into the back room. I wondered what she and Linda talked about. How did they have anything in common?

The sound of crinkling paper made me look down. I realized I had the flyer in a death grip. Maybe I should go to this concert. I was a sporting-event type of girl, not a loud-music event one. At least that's what I had always thought. But here I was standing in this store, in these clothes, hearing the sound of laughter in the back room, and realizing that maybe there was more to me than I realized.

CHAPTER 18

• • • • • • •

Just because I decided I would go to the concert didn't mean I had to go alone. I impulsively called Amber to go with me. I figured she was more the rock-concert type than anyone else I knew.

She was on her way to my house, but I was up in my bedroom, trapped by the sounds of my brothers downstairs. It should've been easy for me to march down there in these clothes that I'd been wearing at work for weeks and tell them I was going out. It wasn't. They still hadn't seen me like this. And I felt like a fraud. Like this was just me playing pretend. Like they'd call me out on that fact.

Their laughter carried into my bedroom even though I had the door tightly shut. They were loud. I looked at my outfit one more time—a pair of skinny jeans and a shirt that showed more of my chest than I was used to showing. My hair hung down my back and actually looked shiny and full today with the help of some tips I'd learned from Amber.

I threw my shoulders back and headed for the door. I could do this. The door handle felt like a weight in my hand, too heavy to turn. Defeat wasn't usually a feeling I let myself live with, but this time I knew I was beat. I walked to my closet, retrieved an oversized sweatshirt, and threw it on. Then I grabbed an elastic band from my desk, pulled my hair back, and went downstairs.

"Charlie!" Gage said the minute I'd reached the landing. "Hurry, get over here. I just bet Braden I could throw five pieces of popcorn into your mouth in under thirty seconds."

"What?"

"Stand over there." He pointed to a spot ten feet in front of him.

I looked at Braden, who was sitting on the couch, his feet on the coffee table. One side of his mouth lifted into a smile. Why did his smile make me want to do this? "He can't do it," Braden said.

"Why am I the person who has to be on the receiving end in this bet?"

Gage shrugged. "I don't know. Braden said it'd be harder or something so I should get you down here. I was just about to text you."

Braden wanted me down here. I looked at him again.

"I didn't want grease on my face," he said, but his cheeks seemed to brighten with a tint of pink. "Just open your mouth. There's money on the line here."

I rolled my eyes. "No, I don't have time for you dorks tonight. I'm going out."

"Where are you going?" Gage asked.

I wanted to tell them where I was going, and if it were just Braden, I might've. But I wasn't ready for questions from Gage. "Work. Inventory." It hurt me to lie to him like that. We were close. I usually told him everything.

"Have fun." I started to walk away, thinking I should just turn around and tell them I was going to a concert. Maybe they'd even want to go with me. But then Gage said, "Braden, go stand over there. I can make five pieces."

"Are you sure you're ready to lose five bucks?"

"Do it."

I looked once over my shoulder as I headed for the door and saw Braden standing up to be the target for Gage's popcorn. Our eyes met for a moment, and normally I would've said something like *You shouldn't have made a bet like that when your mouth is so big.* Or *Popcorn in the eye sounds fun.* But instead I just stared until my foot caught on the edge of the carpet and I pitched forward, nearly falling flat on my face. The sound of laughter behind me propelled me right out the door.

When I jumped into the front seat of Amber's car, I took the elastic band out of my hair, then peeled off my sweatshirt and threw it in the backseat. She pulled away from the curb.

"You're not wearing much makeup."

I usually wore none. But tonight I had applied a coat of mascara and my ChapStick. *I never do* is what I should've told her, but instead I said, "I didn't have time to put a lot on."

"There's a purple case in my bag in the back. You can borrow some." She reached over and flipped down the visor in front of me, revealing a mirror.

An image flashed through my mind of me sitting in the backseat of a car, watching my mom apply makeup. She looked back at me, sunlight turning the outline of her dark hair white, and smiled. Then she put a hand on my knee before going back to her task.

The memory was like a jolt to my mind. I squeezed my eyes shut and flipped the visor back up. "I think I'm okay."

"Okay. Oh, I meant to ask you if you could be the canvas for Antonia. The girl she arranged with fell through, and this is her first class at this store." She opened the center console and pulled out a flyer. "I told her you might do it. I'd do it, but I'm doing my cousin's makeup for her wedding. It's this Sunday."

I took a deep breath, trying to forget the flash of memory, and stared at the flyer, not processing anything. "What time?"

"In the afternoon, I think. Doesn't it say on there?"

It did. "Sure. I just have church in the morning, but we're done by eleven, so this will work."

"Thank you. She'll be so relieved."

Amber found a parking spot on the street and we hopped out. Even before we got to the doors, the music poured out of the building and into the night. The place was crowded and the energy of the people pushed against me as we made our way inside. I wasn't used to feeling so much excitement buzzing outside of a sporting event. I wasn't sure what to do with it. Normally I'd run or push back or charge. This wasn't exactly the place for that. The group in the middle of the club was jumping up and down to the beat of the song. Maybe I needed to be in there.

The music went quiet, though, and the guy onstage announced that the next band would be out in five minutes. I hoped we hadn't missed the one Skye wanted me to see—her boyfriend's band. After searching for a while, we found Skye toward the back.

"Charlie! You came." She gave me a side hug. "I wasn't sure if you would." She gave my outfit a once-over. "You look cute."

"Thanks."

"Not that I'm surprised. You have killer style."

I let out a laugh but was surprised when neither she nor Amber laughed along. So that wasn't a joke.

"Oh, look, Toad's back on," Skye said.

"Toad?" I asked.

"Henry." She gestured toward the stage. "It's a nickname my friend gave him and it's stuck."

"Is that why they named themselves The Crusty Toads?"

"No, actually. The nickname came second."

I'd had a lot of nicknames in my life. "Toad" wasn't any worse than "Charles Barkley," which was what my brothers called me sometimes.

"Who's the singer?" Amber asked. "He's dreamy."

"Mason," Skye said, then leaned closer so we could hear her over the music. "So I was talking to Linda the other day, Charlie, and she showed me your pictures. They were great."

"She did? Sorry you had to suffer through that. She's just proud."

"Of course she is. She's going to be your Mama Lou

soon too," Skye said, giving me a wink.

My mind flashed back to the image of my mom in the car, smiling at me. "She's not going to be my mom."

I must've said it with an edge, because Skye's eyes widened. "I didn't mean your real mom. I just meant that she's everyone's mom."

My skin itched. "I think I'm going to go dance for a while." I pointed to the group in the center of the room. I needed to burn off the stagnant energy hanging around me.

"Me too," Amber said, trailing after me.

Dancing wasn't quite the same as running . . . or any sport, for that matter. I didn't feel like I had a purpose, a goal. But after a while I let my mind relax and realized not everything had to have a point. Some things could just be for the fun of it. I looked over at Amber dancing next to me. She smiled, then hooked her arm in mine and twirled me around. My surroundings blurred and I soaked the moment in, deciding this night was something I could do again.

CHAPTER 19

• • • • • • •

The makeup venue for Antonia was bigger than Linda's store. The word must've gotten around about these demos because there were more people, too. Probably close to fifty. I wove through groups until I got to the front and found a slightly panicked Antonia.

She grabbed my arm, relief flooding her eyes. "I thought you weren't going to show."

"I'm sorry. Am I late?" I glanced at my cell, which showed I had a ten-minute cushion.

"No. I'm just nervous. There are so many people. I guess there's a bridal show in town this weekend and all these brides are here."

I looked around and saw lots of white. "Oh, this is a bridal store."

She laughed. "Yes. I'm showcasing the bridal line today."

"Okay. Where do you want me?"

She pointed to a high stool and I positioned myself in the seat. A man in a suit walked up and introduced himself as the owner of the store. "The photographer will be here soon to get some photos of the session."

"Photos?"

He opened a folder he held, then ran a finger down the first page. "I got your parental waiver for that, right? You're . . ."

Antonia went wide-eyed from where she stood slightly behind him. "Chloe. She's Chloe." She gave me a pleading look.

"Right," I said. "I'm Chloe."

"Right. Here you are. Thanks." He walked away.

"I'm sorry," Antonia said. "I forgot about the stupid waiver he told Chloe to bring in when I thought she was doing it. Thanks for covering for me. It's just so he can take pictures for the portfolio that will be next to the display in the store. Are you okay with that?"

"It's fine."

She must've thought I didn't mean that, because she

kept going. "It's not really a big deal. Mostly extreme close-ups anyway, of, like, your eyes or your lips. No one will know it's you."

Extreme close-ups were not a good way to sell anything. But I knew what she meant. "It's fine," I said again.

She squeezed my arm. "Thank you."

Antonia wasn't kidding about extreme close-ups. It felt like the photographer was inches from my face throughout the session, taking pictures as Antonia progressed through the stages. I was seeing stars from the flash by the time it was over.

As the last people left, Antonia turned to me and blew air between her lips in an expression of relief. "I'm so glad that's over. It was way harder in real life than in practice."

I laughed. Now *that* I could relate to. My nerves were always way more intense at an actual game than during practice.

"Let me buy you dinner for bailing me out."

I smiled. "Sounds fun."

It was late when I got home. I was still fully made up (Antonia didn't have makeup wipes like Amber did), I could feel the foundation thick on my face, and my eyelashes were heavy with mascara. Plus my hair was down because I'd forgotten to bring an elastic. I needed to get in the house unseen.

I stealthily walked the front path to my house. The window next to the front door was dark, so I let myself relax as I slid the key in the lock and eased the front door open. Gage reclined on the couch, watching television, and he looked over at me with a nod—then did a double take, seeming to take a moment to process my identity.

"I just had some very unclean thoughts about my sister go through my head. I feel disgusting now."

I offered a weak smile of apology.

"You look different." He pointed to his own hair and face. "Are you wearing crap all over your face? I shouldn't be worried that you work in the red-light district at night, right?"

I wadded up my sweatshirt and threw it at his head. Since his question was rhetorical as far as I was concerned, I continued upstairs, grabbed my pajamas, and then jumped in the shower.

I scrubbed at the makeup on my face, wanting it gone. At home, that other part of my life seemed so foreign.

When I emerged, I found Gage sitting on my bed, along with Nathan.

I rolled my eyes.

"She doesn't look any different to me," Nathan said.

Gage shook his head and pointed at my face. "Her

hair was wavy or something and she was wearing lots and lots of makeup. Her eyelashes and her lips and her cheeks—"

"Gage. Out."

"Not until you explain."

"Ugh. It's nothing. I've just been the mannequin for a makeup line." I thought about my choice of words and the stupid mannequin in Linda's store. I felt like that lately—like all my pieces had been taken off and put back together lopsided.

"What?" Nathan asked. Then he looked to Gage when I didn't answer. "What does that mean?"

"Do you mean modeling? You've been modeling?" Gage asked.

"Not really. Just sitting there while a girl puts makeup on me. Now get out before I beat you both."

"Does Dad know?"

I groaned. "No. And he doesn't need to." He'd die if he knew I'd been lying to him about this. They both looked at me skeptically. "Can I buy your silence? I'll give you each fifty bucks if neither of you says another word about this."

"What are you, Ms. Money Bags now? Exactly what kind of modeling are you doing?"

"Oh. My. Gosh. Get out."

Gage pointed to my dresser in a lightbulb moment.

"That girl. Amber. You really do know her. You work with her."

"Your brilliance knows no bounds." This time I grabbed him by the arm and dragged him to the door. Nathan followed willingly. Before he left, Nathan turned back and said, "If you don't tell Dad, you know I'll have to."

"Of course I know that, Nathan. You've never broken a rule in your life. Are your insides twisting up right now with my secret?" It was supposed to be a joke, but my insides were the ones all twisted up.

Nathan smiled but didn't deny my accusation.

Gage, whose arm I still held and who I was trying to shove out the door, finally stepped out, but not before he said, "Since when do you keep secrets from me?" The way he said it, and the sadness in his eyes, hurt. Before I could defend myself, he'd walked away.

CHAPTER 20

· · · · · · ·

I tossed and turned until the clock read midnight. I slid out of bed and padded to the bathroom, where I splashed cold water on my face. I leaned into the counter and stared at my bloodshot eyes. Water dripped down my face and onto the counter. I grabbed a towel and patted it dry.

Downstairs, I pulled out the box of pictures my dad kept in a drawer beneath the coffee table. I flipped slowly through the ones of my mother. I wanted them to tell me something different. Something they'd never told me before. Clues about her life. Her personality. But they didn't. They just told me what they always did.

She was beautiful. People said I looked like her, and maybe our faces resembled each other, but her body was wispy and soft. Even in pictures I could tell she was graceful. Maybe she could've taught me to be graceful. I wondered if she would have been disappointed with a sporty daughter. Or maybe she'd have been disappointed in who I'd become lately—a liar and a fake.

I tucked the pictures back in the box and headed to my room. The light was off, so the first thing I saw when I walked in was my lit-up cell phone. It was a text from Braden: *Are you awake?*

Yes. On my way out.

"Everything okay?" I asked him at the fence.

He didn't answer for several beats. "Fine."

"Braden. Don't lie to me."

He sighed. "It's just the same old stuff. What's the point in talking about it?"

"Your dad?"

"Yes."

I bit my bottom lip, not sure how to help him with this. "Why don't you talk to him?"

"About what?"

"I don't know. About how he is with you and your mom."

"It won't help."

"Have you tried?"

"No. But my mom tries all the time. You've heard the results."

"I'm sorry."

"Eh." He shrugged with that sound. I couldn't see it, but I knew it well. "It could be worse. What about you? Why are you up so late? More nightmares?"

"Yes."

"Are they getting worse?"

Yes. "I don't know."

"You said before that sometimes you dream about the car accident. What happens in those dreams?"

I thought back. It was definitely the dream I had the most. "Different things every time. I basically just see my mom's crash. Glass. Blood." And I didn't want to talk about this anymore. "My brothers found out something I didn't want them to tonight and now I have to tell my dad something I don't want to tell him."

"Please be more vague. I think you're speaking too clearly."

"I've been modeling makeup." I coughed out the word, and he had to ask me to repeat it twice.

"Modeling?"

"In the loosest sense of the word."

"And why can't you tell your dad?"

"I could've at first. But I didn't. And now it's like I've

been lying to him. He'll wonder why. He'll think it's a bigger deal than it is. He'll think I've gone off the deep end."

"Have you?"

I laughed.

"I want to see."

"See what?"

"You at work."

I thought about it. Showing the disembodied Braden might not be so bad . . . but . . . the real Braden . . . "No, I can't, it's too weird. It feels so outside of myself when I do that. And then when I see myself I feel like I'm looking at someone who isn't even me. It's like the anti-me. Almost as if I have two lives."

"Sometimes I feel like that."

"Yeah?"

"This life, our fence life. And then our day life."

"I know what you mean."

"Why do we do that? Why do we pretend during the day that this doesn't happen?" Our backs must've been perfectly aligned against the fence tonight because I could feel his voice vibrating through the board between us.

I thought about his question, wondered why I couldn't talk about this during the day with him. "Because this is like a dream. It doesn't have to be real. It almost feels like we're floating just outside of consciousness and we can say whatever we want, and in the morning, like with dreams, it just slowly melts away. It's like you're up in your bed sleeping and I'm in mine and our subconscious minds are talking."

"And the daytime me . . . the conscious one . . . you don't like that version?"

"What? No. Of course not. I love that version. That's my Braden. I don't want to lose that to this sniveling version of myself."

"There's nothing at all sniveling about you, Charles."

"But your subconscious knows I'm weaker out here at night, because you started calling me that."

"What?"

"Charles. That's the name you called me when we were little."

"No, if you remember right, that's the name I called you when we talked more. We used to talk more."

I could usually picture Braden's expressions in my mind when we talked like this, but right now I couldn't. His voice sounded even, almost expressionless, so I couldn't tell how he felt about what he'd just said.

"I know. What happened?"

"Gage."

"What?"

"You grew up, and then Gage would look at me funny

when I would search you out or when we'd join him after having been alone together. I felt like his looks were his way of saying 'It's time to distance yourself from my sister.'"

"Really?" This was news to me.

"I think he didn't quite trust me. He thought I had ulterior motives." Again, his expressionless voice was leaving me blind to how he felt about all this.

And did you? I wanted to ask. But that question wouldn't come out. There was too much to lose with that question. "He trusts you. You're like our brother."

"But you're their sister."

"And yours."

"You're not my sister, Charlie. And they know that. They are very protective of you. More than you could possibly know."

"What's that supposed to mean?" It sounded so cryptic.

"You said this is our alternate reality, right? Where we can say anything?"

I was wary. "Yes."

"I need to tell you something. . . . I think it might help. . . ." He stopped. "But I need to come over there to do it." Without waiting for my reply, he had hopped the fence and his disembodied voice stood above me, very much bodied. Now I understood why his voice had sounded emotionless—because his eyes had claimed all the emotion. They were so intense that my heart leaped in my chest.

I stood and backed up against the fence. "Wow, you should be a high jumper. Did you ever try that at school?" If I just pretended like this was normal maybe my heart would stop trying to escape. I didn't want things to change. I didn't want him to tell me whatever had him standing in front of me with fire in his eyes. He was my friend. My best friend, I realized. There was too much to lose.

"No. I didn't."

"You should, with hops like that. That fence is, what, eight feet high, and I'm sure you didn't leap off the ground or anything but—"

"Charlie."

"Did you put one foot on the fence or did you rely on your hands to help you over? Because—"

"Please, Charlie, I can't keep this inside me any longer. You need to know."

"Stop. I don't want to know." I pushed my palms to my eyes. Too many unfamiliar things were happening to me lately, and I didn't need him to add to it.

He grabbed my wrists, taking my hands away from my eyes. "Don't hide from this. You already know. You have to know."

"I don't."

"Think, Charlie."

He dropped my wrists, and I was so nervous that I needed something to hang on to. I pressed both hands against his chest. I could feel his pecs through the thin fabric, his heart beating wildly.

"You know." It wasn't a question.

"I think, but I don't want to." I didn't want to lose him as a friend. Not now, when I needed him the most. I didn't know how I felt right now about anything. I knew I wasn't completely myself. I felt off. And that wasn't fair to him. Now wasn't the time to try to figure out how I felt about him, when I didn't even know how I felt about me.

"It's time. You're older now. It can only help things. They don't think it's a good idea, but you're strong, I know you can handle it."

Now I was confused. "Who doesn't think it's a good idea?"

"Your brothers."

"It's none of their business."

"Of course it is."

"They can't tell you to stop having feelings for me."

He froze mid-nod. "What?" A ripple of confusion ran down his face, and then a light of understanding. He took a step back, my hands slipping from his chest. "I . . . no. That's not what this is about. Is that what you thought I was trying to tell you?" He put a hand to his forehead. "Man, I'm sorry. No, this is about something completely different. . . ."

I squeezed my eyes shut and wiped my hands on my thighs. "I'm such an idiot." With an uncomfortable laugh I said, "Good thing this took place in our dream world so that tomorrow won't be incredibly awkward." I side-stepped around him and headed for the house.

"No, wait, Charlie, please."

I lifted my hand in a silent good-bye without turning around, then let the door shut behind me. Of course Braden didn't like me like that. I was his buddy, his pal, his sister. A burly girl who played sports. The only way a guy would ever like me was with a thick layer of makeup. Not that it mattered. I didn't like him like that either. Well, maybe I had for a second, but he'd just made those feelings easier to resist.

CHAPTER 21

• • • • • • •

The next day, and the day after that, Braden didn't come by the house. It was the longest he'd ever stayed away. Quite obviously he was avoiding me. It was fine with me because I was avoiding him, too. I felt like the biggest idiot. I thought that feeling might go away after a few days. But if anything, the more time passed, the stupider I felt. What had he wanted to tell me that night anyway? Why hadn't I forced him to talk about it? Maybe because I didn't want to know. It seemed serious. What if he had talked his mom into leaving his dad and now he was leaving with her? I didn't like that thought. I didn't want

Braden leaving. No. That was selfish. If it meant he'd be happier, then of course he needed to go. The thought made my heart twist.

I tried to solve the tension by running more, sometimes even twice a day. It felt good to open my lungs and let my legs work out the energy bouncing through my body. On the fourth day after The Talk of Shame, I walked into the kitchen after a long run and saw Braden and Gage sitting at the bar.

"Hey, losers." I could pretend nothing happened. It had been a fence chat, after all. I grabbed a cold water bottle from the fridge and took several large gulps.

"Braden and I were just discussing the fact that Amendola was picked up by the Patriots. I think it means they are the strongest team in the league because of the quarterback–wide receiver duo. It will be like Montana and Rice all over again. But Braden thinks the Rodgers–Cobb duo is still the strongest. Break the tie."

"Neither. Broncos have Manning. End of story."

"One person does not make a team."

"It does if it's Manning."

"Manning is overrated," Gage said.

I splashed some of my water at Gage. "You're overrated." Braden smiled and relief rushed through me. I just wanted things to be normal again. None of this awkward I-jumped-to-stupid-conclusions business. No more thinking about what else he might've wanted to tell me.

"What's wrong?" Gage asked.

"Nothing."

"Didn't you already run once today?" He tilted his head as if he were confused about that, when my cell phone, which was charging on the counter, jumped with an incoming call. Before I could grab it, Gage swiped it up and answered.

"Hello?" A small pause. "What do you mean 'Who's this?'"

I took a sip of water and rolled my eyes. Anybody calling on my cell phone had dealt with my brother before. They'd know he was a jokester.

"Who are you?" Gage asked.

I lifted my toe to stretch my calf when Gage said, "Evan who?" I stopped suddenly, my heart giving an unexpected flip. Oh. Except Evan. He wouldn't know. I held out my hand for the phone.

"I guess that depends," Gage said into the phone, not making even the slightest motion that he intended to give it to me.

"I'm going to murder you, Gage. Give me my phone."

He listened, then stood when he saw me coming around the island to retrieve the phone from him by force. As I passed Braden, about to catch Gage, Braden grabbed me around the waist and held me tight. Because he was sitting down, his face was level with my neck.

"Traitor," I said, smacking him on the head a few times and then struggling to get free. "I hope my stink from running is burning your nostrils right now."

He pressed his nose to my neck and took a big whiff. "Smells like sunshine and rainbows."

I stopped moving as a chill went down my entire body, and forced myself not to shiver with it. Once in control, I grabbed a handful of his hair to pull him away from me, but froze when Gage started talking again.

"And how do you know Charlie?" He gave me a weird look. "A café? Are you sure you have the right Charlie?"

"Gage Joseph Reynolds. I am going to call every girl in your contacts tonight and tell them you are gay." I shoved Braden away from me and he finally let go.

Gage laughed. "Oh, you know what, Charlie just walked in. Here she is."

I punched Gage in the stomach and took two deep breaths. "Hello."

"Hi, Charlie. It's Evan."

A smile took over my face. "Oh. Hi, Evan. How are you?"

"Who was that?"

"My brother. He's a little slow but we love him anyway."

"Hey," Gage yelled. "I'm the smartest one in this house."

I could hear the smile in Evan's voice when he said, "He was obviously trying to irritate you."

"Isn't that what big brothers do?"

"I wouldn't know, I only have one sister and she's five years older than me."

"Ah, well, take my word for it."

He laughed. "So, I was just wondering if you still wanted to go to a baseball game with me, because my dad said we could use his tickets for this Saturday."

"This Saturday!" I realized I had yelled in my excitement, so I cleared my throat and tried to calm my voice. "For sure. I'm in."

"Great. Um . . . there are four tickets, so I thought we could take Dustin with us too. Do you think you can get one of the other girls to come? Amber maybe?"

"Sure. I'll ask her. Where should we meet?"

"I could pick you up. Five, maybe? It takes about an hour and a half to drive up there depending on traffic."

"Sounds good. I'll text you directions. And just a warning: that was only one of my brothers. I have four." Yes, I included Braden in that count, since apparently that's exactly how he saw himself. "And my dad is a cop."

"Wow. Way to make a guy feel at ease."

"You'll be fine. See you Saturday." I hung up the phone, the smile still on my face. There was nothing that made a girl feel better about a guy humiliating her than a different cute guy asking her out.

Behind me, Gage said in a low voice, "He will not be fine." Then he laughed maniacally.

I whirled around. "If you ever do that again, something really bad is going to happen to you."

"As in you are going to do something bad to me, or Fate is going to even the score? I really need to know, because it will make a difference in my decision."

I shook my head.

"Who's Evan?" Braden asked, his hazel eyes on me.

"Someone who is taking me to the A's game this Saturday. And I know you both know who the A's are playing. That's right—the Giants." I sang out a high-pitched note of taunting. "Who's jealous?" I knew Braden was. I knew beyond anything that he would love to go to that game, and I felt terrible. But rubbing it in his face seemed the correct way to deal with those feelings.

Gage went to the kitchen drawer beneath the phone and pulled out a paper and pen. "Okay, you'll need to write his full name here so Dad can run a background check."

I sighed. "No."

"How did you meet him? Where does he go to school?

How old is he? Is he even an A's fan?"

"Pretty sure he's an A's fan, since he has season tickets."

"Call him back and ask if he has any extra," Gage said.

"He does, but those are for my other friends. So tough luck."

"Isn't What's-his-name's wedding on Saturday anyway?" Braden asked.

"Who's What's-his-name?" I asked. "Wait, did I forget about some lame wedding I'm supposed to be at?"

Gage waved me off. "No. It's this guy we know from years and years of soccer camp. He's a couple of years older than Jerom."

I pointed at Braden. "But obviously you don't know him or you'd actually know What's-his-name's name."

"I never went to soccer camp, Charlie."

"I know." Hadn't we established I knew his life pretty well? "Soccer camp people do actually leave soccer camp at some point, though."

Gage interrupted any comeback Braden might've come up with by saying, "His name is Ryan, and you're right, his wedding is Saturday. Crap. How are we supposed to humiliate Charlie's date?" He patted Braden on the shoulder. "Looks like it's all on you, my brother. Make us proud."

"I'll do my best."

Gage got up to leave, Braden trailing after him.

"Please don't do anything to Evan," I said to Braden as he reached the door.

He turned back. "No worries. I'll steer clear."

"Thanks." If only I believed him.

CHAPTER 22

• • • • • • •

I came home from my shift at the store on Saturday just in time to see my brothers all tuxed-out for the wedding. "Look who cleans up nice," I said.

"You're one to talk," Gage mumbled.

"Have fun," I said, bounding upstairs. I only had about two hours before Evan would show up at my door, and I hadn't exactly planned what I was going to wear yet. Last time Evan saw me, I was wearing my work clothes and more makeup than I had ever worn in my life. I knew I wasn't going to replicate that, but I had no idea how far back I wanted to scale it.

My phone rang and I picked it up. "Hello?"

"Hey, Charlie, it's Amber. So I bought a really cute A's jersey to wear to the game because I had no idea what to wear to something like this. And then I wondered if that's what I should wear and I didn't want to feel stupid being the only one wearing an A's jersey."

She honestly thought it possible that she'd be the only one wearing an A's jersey at an A's game?

"So I bought one for you, too. They aren't the same because I didn't want to be twinsies or anything, but they were kind of boring so I bedazzled them."

Bedazzled? What the heck was a bedazzle?

"I hope that's okay. What do you think?"

"That's cool. Jerseys are good. Thanks. How much do I owe you?"

"No, nothing. It's on me."

"Are you sure? Jerseys are expensive."

"I'm sure. When do you want me to come over? I could come over soon and we can get ready together. Do you want me to, or would you rather I just come over right before the guys are going to come get us?"

"Yeah, why don't you come over. I haven't decided what to do with my face yet. You can help me."

I heard her clap. "Yay. I'll bring my makeup case."

And when she said "makeup case," she meant a large briefcase contraption that opened up and then expanded even further with different layers and pullouts.

"Just more natural this time, okay?" After all, my dad was downstairs. He'd see me.

"Of course. This is a baseball game, not a night at the club."

"Right."

She got to work right away on my face.

"What are you going to do with your hair?" she asked.

"I was just going to throw it back in a ponytail."

"Yeah, that will be cute. Then our hair won't take away from our awesome shirts."

"True." She hadn't yet shown me these supposedly awesome shirts, but I was beginning to feel nervous about them. And I was right to feel that way, because when she revealed them I learned that *bedazzling* meant turning something cool into a glittering atrocity. My mouth hung open for a full minute while I took in the glowing gold *A* on the green V-neck jersey.

"I know, awesome, right?" she said, throwing it to me, then stripping off her shirt and putting her own jersey on. Hers was black with a silver *A*. There was no way out of wearing this and I knew it. So instead, I took off the shirt I wished I were wearing and put on the bedazzled jersey, thanking whatever form of good luck had made it possible for my brothers to be gone at What's-his-name's wedding.

"You look so good," Amber said.

She did a full circle, and I realized that girl code

required me to return the compliment. "Yeah, you too."

My phone rang and I picked it up. "Hello?"

"Charlie, hey, it's Evan."

"Hi. What's up?" I glanced at the digital clock on my nightstand. It was four thirty.

"Bad news."

For a millisecond I hoped he was calling to cancel so I could take off this shirt.

"Dustin is sick. Like, beyond sick. Vomiting and the whole works. I've been trying for the last hour to find a replacement with no luck. Do you think one of your brothers can go with us instead?"

"My brothers are at a wedding. . . ." I stopped and looked at Amber, who was checking out the back of her shirt in my mirror, a big smile on her face. "I'll find someone."

"Are you sure?"

"Yeah. See you in half an hour."

"Sorry," he said as he hung up.

"I'll be right back," I told Amber.

In the hall, I put the phone to my ear and listened to it ring three times.

"Hello?"

"Braden."

"You don't need to give me any threatening speeches. I really wasn't planning to bug your date at all tonight."

"The fact that you remembered I have a date makes

me doubt that entirely." Wait, why did he remember? Did it bother him? No. That didn't matter. We were friends. "But actually, I have the best news ever. You will love me for eternity."

"Uh-oh."

"It's not a bad thing."

"Okay. What do I have to do?"

"One of our friends got violently ill today. . . ."

"Wow, that *is* good news."

I laughed. "Well, I guess that's not good news. But his ill fortune is your gain, because he can't go to the game. Do you want to come with us?"

"To the A's game?" I could hear the excitement in his voice.

"Yeah."

"So am I replacing a guy or a girl?"

"A guy. Dustin. His date is Amber. She's hot. Another reason you should be forever indebted to me." I couldn't believe I was doing this. I was setting up Braden with Amber. He really would fall for her. This was a good thing, I told myself. Exactly what I needed to happen so that Braden and I could maintain the amazing friendship we'd had for years.

He laughed. "All right. You twisted my arm."

"Be over in half an hour."

CHAPTER 23

• • • • • • •

My dad stared at me like I was speaking another language. I was convinced he had gotten over the initial shock of seeing me in makeup and a bedazzled shirt and had now moved on to trying to process what I was telling him. "Why didn't you mention you were driving to Oakland before now? That's kind of a big deal, Charlie."

"I don't know. I didn't think you'd care. It's the A's game, Dad. Come on." I hoped Amber, who was still upstairs putting the finishing touches on her hair, couldn't hear us.

"Well, I do care."

We each took a deep breath. My hands clenched into
fists. He looked at me again and his face softened a little.
He closed his eyes and when he opened them he said,
"You look so much like her."

My heart stuttered in my chest. So that was what the
initial shock was about. With makeup on, I looked more
like my mom. It was the wrong time for this, but my
whole body waited anxiously for him to say something
else. He didn't. Instead, that familiar look of guilt filled
his eyes. The one that said he wished someone else was
in charge of me, because he had no idea what to do with
me and this situation, and he felt bad about it. I hesitated,
then said, "Is that why you're so nervous to let me go?
Because I'll be driving a long distance in a car? We'll be
safe."

His brows shot down. "No, Charlie. That's not why.
This is nothing like that."

How was this nothing like that? My mom died in a
car accident and now he was worried about me driving
an hour and a half in a car. It didn't seem so different to
me. He glanced up the stairs like he, too, realized this
was a bad time, with Amber steps away. He pinched the
bridge of his nose and the guilt look turned into a sad
look. Great, now I had him thinking about my mom.
Stupid makeup.

"I'll call and check in with you every hour. You can

even have a police car tail us if you want."

That suggestion made him smile a little, but he still said, "I just don't feel comfortable with it."

"Dad, you'll like Evan. He's really responsible and nice and . . ." I couldn't think of any other adjectives for Evan since I hardly knew him. I wasn't even sure if the first adjective described him. So, yeah, this wasn't my most brilliant idea ever.

I heard the door open and shut behind me, and my dad looked over.

"Hey, Mr. R," Braden said.

I tightened my ponytail and sighed, because I'd suddenly realized after all this my dad wasn't going to let me go.

"Nice shirt, Charlie," Braden said, tugging on the back, probably taking in each gaudy fake jewel.

"Yeah, Amber made it."

"I hope you don't blind the pitcher with the bling coming off this thing, because I don't want any pitchers mad at me tonight."

"Wait." My dad pointed at Braden. "You're going?"

"Yes."

I could actually see the muscles in my dad's jaw relax. "Why didn't you say so, Charlie?"

Why *didn't* I say so? I should've known that would make a difference. "I don't know. So we can go?"

"Yes. Be careful and call me when you're heading home."

"Thanks." I turned around and mouthed *Thank you* to Braden as well. His eyes went wide. "What?" I asked, but then remembered how different I must've looked in a fitted V-neck jersey and more makeup than I normally wore. "Don't say a word. I know I look like a clown."

He shook his head back and forth. "No. You look . . . different."

"Thanks for the confidence boost."

"Sorry. It's not bad." He looked at my shirt, then up to my face again. "It's just not you."

"Two lives, remember?" It was the closest I'd come to referencing our fence talks during the day. "Oh, don't look now, here comes your hot date." I watched Amber come down the stairs, and even I knew she was beautiful. Bedazzled shirt and all. In fact, she kind of owned the bedazzled shirt.

Braden smiled his beautiful crooked smile at her, and I watched as her expression beamed pleasant surprise. She hadn't been happy when I first told her, but I convinced her that Braden would be a way better date than Dustin. And now, looking at Braden and imagining how it would be to see him for the first time, like she was, I realized how gorgeous he was. His auburn hair flopped onto his forehead in a boyish way, but there was nothing boyish about him. He had grown up, filled out, matured. His shoulders were broad, his jaw strong.

I watched the two of them come together and smile shyly at one another. A pang of jealousy radiated through my chest.

I brushed away those unhelpful feelings as he shook Amber's hand and introduced himself. This was going to be hard. I shouldn't have invited him. Five minutes later, the doorbell rang and I opened the door. Evan greeted me with a smile that wasn't anywhere near as familiar as Braden's. "You look beautiful," he said.

He looked short. Our first and only meeting had been at the café, sitting around the booth. I didn't realize how tall he was at the time, but we were basically eye to eye. Granted, I was five-eleven and was surrounded by people over six-three in my everyday life, so I wasn't used to average.

"Thanks. Come in. My dad wants to meet you."

He took a deep breath as if preparing for the encounter.

"Dad, this is Evan."

My dad grabbed his hand in a firm shake. "Drive knowing that if anything happens to my daughter in your car, I will hold you personally responsible."

"Dad."

"I will, sir."

"Good." He finally released his hand.

I managed to hold back an eye roll. "Okay, we'll see you later."

As we were leaving, I noticed my dad clamp his hand onto Braden's shoulder and say something under his breath. Braden smiled and nodded, and then my dad gave him a friendly pat on the back. "Have fun," he said.

"What was that all about?" I asked Braden when we left the house.

"Oh, you know, protecting-Charlie instructions."

"Funny."

Braden gave Evan, who was walking down the path in front of us, a once-over. It wasn't until Braden paused on Evan's loafers that I realized he was wearing them. Braden raised his eyebrows at me and I nearly laughed.

Evan slowed his walk so that Braden and I caught up. "I'm Evan."

"Oh, sorry," I said, realizing I hadn't introduced them. "This is Braden. Braden, this is Evan."

They shook hands, and we resumed our walk to the car. Once we got there, we all stood for a second—each, I was sure, trying to figure out seating arrangements for the long drive.

"Girls in the back?" I suggested, not sure what date protocol was.

"I'll sit in the back," Braden said. "Why don't you take shotgun, Charlie?"

"Are you sure? There's more leg room up there."

Amber gave me a withering look that seemed to say *Let him sit in the back with me.*

"I'm sure," he said, and I wondered if he was just as excited as Amber about the close quarters.

I nodded, and they climbed into the back as Evan opened the door for me.

"You're tall," he said just as I started to get in. It was hard to tell if he was disappointed that I was tall or happy about it. So I just climbed in without a word.

At moments like these, I was grateful for Amber's chatty nature. She kept the conversation in the car flowing naturally. Once there, I watched Braden's reaction as we walked into the stadium. His eyes lit up and seemed to take in every detail, committing them to memory. It was pretty awe-worthy. Years of watching baseball on television did not prepare me for how beautiful and big the Coliseum would be. The grass was greener than any I had ever seen and the bases glowed white. Rows upon rows of green plastic seats filled the cement steps.

Evan laughed next to me. "You look starstruck."

"It's amazing."

We worked our way down to seats that were fairly close, right next to first base. I nudged Braden's arm so we could share a this-is-so-awesome look. He smiled at me, then squeezed my hand once. The gesture surprised

me, and just when I was about to look up at Braden to
see if there was any hint in his eyes as to what it meant,
Evan put his arm around my shoulders and pointed to
the home team dugout. "That's where the A's will sit."

I nodded as though he was imparting some sort of
new wisdom to me.

"You see that net thing? That's where the pitcher
warms up."

"She's not an idiot," Braden said. "She knows what a
practice screen is."

I shot Braden a look as we all took our seats. Amber
and I ended up sitting next to each other with the guys on
the outside. Probably a good thing, considering Braden's
previous remarks. I found myself slouching down a little
so that I didn't sit taller than Evan.

"I'm thirsty," Amber said the minute we sat down.
"Charlie and I are going to go get some drinks before the
game starts." She pulled me up by my arm.

"Okay. Guess we're going to get some drinks. Do you
want anything?" I asked Evan.

He reached in his pocket and pulled out a twenty.
"Yes, will you get me a Dr Pepper?"

"Sure."

Amber looked at Braden.

"No, I'm good." And then, as if he remembered he
was supposed to be her date, he quickly retrieved some

money from his wallet and handed it to her.

She smiled her brightest smile. "Thanks." The thing that bothered me was that the only reason I took Evan's money was because he ordered a soda. I fully intended to pay for my own. So now I felt bad because I shamed Braden into giving Amber money.

As we walked up the steps to the concession stands, Amber said, "Geez, Charlie, when you were going on and on about how nice and funny and sweet Braden was, I thought he must be dog-ugly because you were focusing so much on his personality. All you had to say was he was hot and I would've been sold."

I nodded, trying my hardest not to be bothered. There was so much more to Braden than his looks. "Yeah, I've known him my whole life, so I know him really well."

"Do you think he likes me?"

He better not. "He just met you."

"But don't you believe in Fate? I mean, here I was supposed to go out with Dustin and suddenly he gets sick and who should happen to take his place but the man of my dreams? It must be fate."

"Must be."

"I'm going to buy him a drink anyway," she said as we reached the front of the line. "What's his favorite?"

Don't you mean he is going to buy himself a drink? I wanted to say, but I decided I was being unfair to her just because she was Braden's date. I was the one who invited him to begin with. Did I honestly think Amber wouldn't find him attractive and vice versa? "He's not really into soda, actually. Get him water or Gatorade and he'll be happy."

When she ordered a cherry Gatorade, I kept my mouth shut at first, knowing that was his least favorite. Cherry-flavored anything reminded him of cough medicine. But finally, I felt guilty enough to say "Lemon is his favorite."

"Thanks." She smiled at me with her perfectly straight, even teeth and changed the order. The way I was acting was not okay. I needed to snap out of it. We were friends. This was what we had both decided. Nothing more. And since when did I begrudge Braden a gorgeous, fun girl? I thought back. It had been a while since I'd seen him with a girl at all. Sure, he had his random dates here and there, but he hadn't had a girlfriend for over a year now. I hadn't been upset back then. I wouldn't be upset now. Because we were friends.

CHAPTER 24

• • • • • • • •

Amber spent the entirety of the game asking Braden questions about the rules and regulations of baseball, playing the perfect example of making a guy feel useful. I spent the entirety of the game pretending to be interested in Evan giving me the play-by-play while trying to actually watch the game. Toward the end of the game, Amber asked how long one of the pitchers had been on the team. "He looks so young," she said.

Braden leaned forward and said, "You know, I'm not sure about that, but Charlie was just telling me about him the other day. How long has he been on the team again?"

I didn't know all the players' entry dates, but I happened to know his and yes, he was young. They all looked at me. The announcer's voice rang out over the loudspeaker: "At the plate is Dunning and on deck is Lopez."

"Um, yeah. He's twenty-four. This is his second year."

"She probably knows his stats, too," Braden said. "She's like a baseball encyclopedia." He leaned back as if his job were done. And his job *was* done—I was mad.

"You should've said something," Evan said. "I've probably been boring you to death."

"No, not at all." I gave him a weak smile. Just being here at the game was more than I could've hoped for. And despite the grade-school lesson on baseball, I was enjoying myself. Or was, until Braden made me feel like a jerk. I knew he did it on purpose, too. I saw the smug look in his eye as he leaned back.

"It's pretty impressive that a girl that looks like you knows so much about baseball."

I heard Braden laugh a little and wanted to punch him. Just because he didn't find me attractive didn't mean he had to make me feel stupid that someone else did. "You want to walk around before the last inning?" I asked.

"Sure," Evan said, standing up and holding out his hand. I took it and tried to convince myself it wasn't just to make Braden mad. Although I had no idea why it would. Except for the fact that maybe he didn't think Evan measured up to the impossible standards he and my brothers set for my dates—he was wearing loafers, after all.

Evan made it past Braden's legs just fine as we walked down the aisle to exit the row, but I knocked into one knee, nearly tripping, and couldn't maneuver around his other. Evan looked back, still holding my hand. I shot Braden a look and he played innocent. I stepped hard on his foot. "Oh, sorry, was that your foot?"

He sucked in air and finally pulled his legs back.

It ended up being a good thing that Braden had outed me (not that I'd thank him anytime soon), because then we talked about things besides baseball. We talked about school and how he wanted to be a financial advisor when he grew up, like his dad. Now, finances were something I knew little to nothing about, so I had all sorts of questions for him. After a while, I said, "Yeah, you lost me when you got into that short-selling-a-stock thing. No idea what you're talking about."

He laughed, and I noticed how amazing it made his eyes look, all lit up like that.

"What's your favorite sport?" I asked.

"To watch or play?"

"Both, I guess."

"I don't know if this counts as a sport to you, but I love to wakeboard."

"Totally counts. That's awesome. So you have a boat?"

"My dad does. He lets us take it out sometimes. Do you ski or wakeboard?"

"I've been a few times, but I'm not very good."

"We should go. I'll give you some pointers."

"That would be really fun. Maybe we could take my brothers. I think you'd like them." And they'd be super impressed if he was good at wakeboarding.

"Yeah, for sure. I'll plan it." He hadn't let go of my hand as we walked around the concession level of the stadium, where they sold nachos, hot dogs, Dippin' Dots, and waffle cones. It felt nice, not even clammy or anything. "Do you want anything to eat?" he asked.

"No, I'm good."

He sighed. "I don't think Braden likes me very much."

"Braden is an idiot," I said. "And he likes you just fine. I think it was me that he was trying to prove a point to." If I didn't know any better, I'd think he was jealous.

"He really looks nothing like you."

"*Oh.* He's not my brother. I'm sorry, I should've clarified that. He's my neighbor. But I've known him for twelve years, so I claim him as a brother, and he's just as annoying as one, so it works out well."

"Oh." He glanced toward where our seats were, as if he could see Braden from here. "Your neighbor."

Evan had a weird expression on his face that I couldn't place.

"Should we head back? The game's almost over," I said, squeezing his hand.

"Yeah."

When we were almost home, Braden said, "So, Evan, what are you doing in the morning?"

"Uh . . . nothing."

"Do you like to play football? It's just a pickup game. We play at nine at the park up the street from our houses."

"Sure, sounds good."

"Ohhh!" Amber squealed. "Do you go, Charlie?"

I nodded, silently seething over the invite.

She grabbed hold of Braden's arm. "Can I come too?"

"Yeah, sure," Braden said. "It's tackle."

I rolled my eyes. Amber wasn't asking to play. She was asking to watch.

Evan hugged me good-bye, and then I watched as he drove away, followed shortly by Amber in her car. Braden and I stood side by side as her taillights disappeared around the corner.

"What was that all about?" he asked.

I took a deliberate step away from him. "What?"

"You pretending like you knew nothing about baseball?"

"That was me being a good date."

He grunted and got that typical look he got when someone said something stupid—chin drawn down, eyes on the verge of rolling. "Really? Because it seemed like that was you playing dumb."

"Whatever. That didn't mean you had to go and do that."

"Do what?"

"Invite him tomorrow."

"Your brothers wanted to meet him. They texted me." He held up his phone, as if that should make me feel better.

I tried to calm down by drawing a deep breath.

"Why are you so mad?" I wasn't a fan of the fact that he could read me so well in that moment.

"Because you just took one of my favorite things away from me."

"I haven't taken anything away from you."

My chest was tight and I had an overwhelming desire to punch him. "I can't play tomorrow. I'll have to sit on the sidelines, cheering you on."

"Why would you have to do that? You're an awesome football player."

"Because, Braden, Evan will be there."

He put on a rare angry face. "If you can't be yourself around him, then you shouldn't be dating him."

I laughed a low mocking laugh. "Oh, yeah, be myself.

Tackle guys, fall in the mud, score touchdowns, that's real appealing to guys."

"It is to some guys."

"Really, Braden? Who? Tell me! Because I've been playing sports with the same ten guys for the last five years of my life and never has one of them hit on me, let alone asked me out. Not one! Do you think any of them see me as someone they would date? Of course they don't. They see me as—let me see, what were the terms you guys used at disc golf the other day? Oh, that's right—a big, burly girl. If they want someone to date, they go to the mall or the club and find a girl who wears tight clothes and does her nails and giggles at their jokes.

"I see the way guys look at Amber. I saw the way *you* looked at Amber. Guys don't want a competitor, they want a cheerleader. So excuse me if I feel like I have to compromise a little of who I am to make a guy"—I pointed up the road—"a cute, nice guy, actually look at me like I'm not his teammate." My eyes stung with anger.

Braden took a step back this time. Then he squeezed his eyes shut before opening them again. "You are so clueless. I don't believe you, the most stubborn girl in the world, would be willing to do that for a guy who's not even worth the time or effort. You don't have to pretend to be anyone else. Your brothers are going to die."

The tension in my chest had built to beyond bearable.

I needed to run or this tension would keep me up all night. That or push him to the ground, which actually sounded fun in that moment. "He's worth *my* time and effort. Good night, Braden," I said, then I ran. Jeans were not fun to run in, but the breathable jersey and the sneakers I always wore made up for it.

I knew Braden had followed me. It was the middle of the night, after all, and he knew my dad would kill him if he let me go alone. I could hear him keeping pace about twenty feet behind me. I hoped he was dying in his jeans and polo shirt. I hoped his Chucks were making the arches of his feet hurt.

The big hill marked the beginning of mile three, and I glanced over my shoulder to see how Braden was holding up. He had slipped another five feet behind. I knew I could lose him over this hill if I wanted to. I could power up the hill and take a different route. But I didn't. By this time my adrenaline had kicked in, easing my tension and making it hard to stay angry. So I slowed down a bit and let him stay within twenty feet, taking a shortcut through the park to make my normally seven-mile run closer to five.

When we got home, Braden, sweat ringing his collar and underarms, just walked into his house without saying a word.

CHAPTER 25

• • • • • • • •

"You don't have to do this," I said to Evan the next morning as we walked from my house to the park, holding hands. "You know what it is, right?"

"I'm proving myself to your brothers or something weird like that?"

"Yeah."

"What about to you? Do I have to prove myself to you?" He smiled and my heart gave a little jump.

"No. Not at all."

Evan had dressed the part this morning—a tee and some breakaway sweats, the snaps by his ankles undone—and I was happy for it. He looked good. He even had on a nice pair of athletic shoes. They were a little too clean, but Braden couldn't possibly complain about them.

"Then I'm fine. I'll just have fun. I may be scrawny, but I enjoy football."

"A lot of the guys are your size. My brothers are just giants."

"Was that supposed to make me feel better?"

"Sorry."

"So I thought Amber was coming too."

"When I texted you guys to just meet at the house, she said she was running late and would meet us at the park."

"Great. I thought another new face would deflect some of the attention off me."

Well, the guys have never seen me in makeup, a fitted shirt, or skinny jeans, so that will probably do the trick, I wanted to say.

I squeezed his hand. "You'll do fine."

Most of the guys were already there setting up cones and throwing the ball around. I got a few odd glances that started on my face and outfit then lingered on Evan's and my clasped hands.

"I take it you don't bring a lot of boys home," Evan whispered.

I just laughed.

My brothers walked over, shoulder to shoulder, and

I felt Evan tense beside me. Gage was the only one with a smile on his face. I wanted to scream in frustration. It was obvious to me now I should've done this more so they didn't act like defensive linemen, ready to take down the quarterback. Seriously, this wasn't my life right now.

"Hey, guys," I said. "Don't be idiots. This is Evan. Evan, the angry-looking one is Jerom, the constipated-looking one is Nathan, and the goofball on the right is Gage."

Gage laughed. "Constipated, Nathan? We said to look fierce." All three of them laughed now, and I relaxed when I realized they were just joking around.

"Good to meet you, Evan," Jerom said, shoving his hand forward.

Evan shook it. I looked around for Braden and saw him on the far side of the field, passing the ball to George. So he was still pouting. I should've been the one ticked at him, not the other way around. He was the one who'd called me not only stubborn but clueless.

"All right," Jerom said, clapping once. "Let's split up into teams. Me and Gage on one side, Nathan and Braden on the other." All four of them played on different teams or the other guys complained. Not just because they were the biggest and the best, but because they all knew each other and could read each other so well that it made an unfair advantage. "Everyone else, pick a side, divide evenly."

"Whose team should I be on?" Evan asked me.

"Jerom and Gage," I said, because I felt like Gage would involve him the most, try the hardest to make him feel welcome. He stepped over to the circle forming around them, and I eased off to the sidelines, waiting for my brothers to realize I wasn't playing.

Gage noticed first and gave me his "What's the deal?" face. I just smiled. Braden shook his head, as if he still didn't believe I wasn't going to participate and now seeing it actually happening made him sick. Finally, Jerom looked over.

"Pick a side, Charlie," he called.

I was saved when a bubbly voice called, "I'm here."

Every head turned to look at Amber. Gage nearly tripped over his own feet. She wore some jeans with flip-flops and a tight black tank top that had sparkly words I couldn't make out written across her chest. It seemed every guy on the field was trying to make out those words too. Her hair was wavy and flowed down around her shoulders.

"Hi, Braden," she called. Now every head turned toward Braden. He blushed a little and then waved.

She had a foldable camping chair flung over one shoulder, and she took it out of its carrying case and set it up next to me. "If I had known you didn't have a chair, I would've brought one for you, too."

"I'm good."

"Do you watch them play a lot?" she asked.

"Yes."

"And you just sit on the ground?"

What was wrong with me? Why couldn't I say that I usually played with them? Because I felt like if I told her that, maybe it would change her opinion of me. I'd be the weird one. The one who played tackle football with guys.

"Are we going to play, or what?" Jerom asked. And with those words, the game started. If I thought they were going to go easy on Evan at all, I was mistaken. Jerom, in his attempts to throw the ball to Evan, pelted him in the chest, the side of the head, and the middle of the back. He was able to catch a few, and that's when Braden would tackle him harder than I'd seen him tackle anyone before. I was itching to play now, so I could get back at them.

Amber hummed beside me. "Geez, Charlie, you didn't tell me your brothers were as pretty as you are."

"What?"

"Your brothers. They're very model-esque, with their gray eyes and high cheekbones. They're beautiful."

"Um . . . Don't let them hear you say that."

"I should've guessed with them being related to you

and all that they'd be striking."

I growled, watching the game. I should've told Evan to be on Braden's team so Braden wouldn't have the opportunity to tackle him like that. "Hold on a minute," I said to Amber, and stood up from where I had been sitting cross-legged on the grass. After the play was over, I marched up to Braden and, not wanting to embarrass Evan, I said in a quiet voice, "Why are you treating a pickup game like the Super Bowl? Unless you want to get some helmets and pads, lay off, Bruiser. If you tackle him like that one more time, we're leaving."

He wouldn't meet my eyes, but the muscle in his jaw was clenched as tight as could be.

"Why are you so mad at me? What is your problem?" I asked.

"You want to know what my problem is?" he asked.

"Yes."

"Are you sure?"

I hesitated now, realizing where we were, but he didn't stop. He took me by the shoulders and turned me around to face the guys, who were now all staring at us. "By a show of hands," Braden said loudly, "who here would've asked Charlie out in the last six months had they not been given the 'We will kill you if you look at Charlie' speech by the three lugs over there when she turned sixteen?"

My first instinct was to yank away from Braden's grip

and never talk to him again. Ever. But the small thread of curiosity weaving through me seemed to have stitched me to the grass, because I couldn't move.

A few of the guys shifted nervously and glanced at Jerom. Just when I started to feel extremely embarrassed that no one had moved, Tyler raised his hand. His bravery seemed to spur the others forward, because at least half a dozen of them put their hands up. Gage, thinking he was hilarious, had even raised his hand. Braden, I noticed, had both hands still firmly grasping my shoulders.

"Which is exactly why we gave the speech," Jerom said darkly.

"You don't have to change for a guy," Braden said quietly in my ear.

If he thought in some way I'd be touched by this public humiliation, he was wrong. "Thanks, Oprah, I'll try to remember that." I looked at Evan. "You ready to go?"

He nodded, rubbing his neck.

CHAPTER 26

• • • • • • •

I waved good-bye to Amber, and she didn't seem at all upset about me abandoning her. I gave Evan a once-over as we walked home. He had a red mark on the side of his neck and one on his bicep—probably from being pelted with the football. A long scratch ran across the back of his hand. Football wasn't a bruise-free kind of sport, but he looked more beaten-up than normal after a pickup game.

"We have a hot tub," I said. "That might help."

"Not sure I want your brothers coming home and finding me in a hot tub with you. See, I didn't get the

'We will kill you' speech, and I'm realizing why guys might steer clear of you if they had. They're like a force, the four of them."

"They are, aren't they?" I sighed. "But they'll be playing for a while longer, so come on. I'll find you some swim shorts, get you a couple aspirin, and we'll relax."

"I'm only agreeing because this means I get to see you in a swimsuit."

I blushed and nudged his shoulder with mine.

Up in my room, after finding him one of Gage's suits and sending him to the bathroom to change, I pulled on my one-piece. He was going to be sorely disappointed. I only wore swimsuits for sport, so it was a pretty boring one.

We met in the hall in an awkward sort of "Do we hold hands on the way to the pool?" exchange that ended with his hand on my lower back. I tried not to stare at his defined chest and abs. So I kept my eyes straight ahead, even though I kind of wanted to see if he had any more welts from the game. No, I wouldn't look; I was already angry enough at Braden.

I turned on the jets in the hot tub and we slid in.

"So . . . ," Evan said after a few moments of silence. "Did I fail miserably?"

"No. You were fine. Really."

"I'm not a huge football player. If it were baseball, I

would've given a much better showing." His hand found mine under the water and grabbed it, playing with my fingers.

"You don't need to excuse yourself over a stupid pickup game. My brothers were going hard on you."

"Your brothers were fine. . . . It was Braden who had a problem with me."

"No. He doesn't have a problem with you. We got in a fight last night. He was angry with me and taking it out on you."

"Maybe. But it's more than that."

"What do you mean?"

"I think he's jealous."

"Of what?"

"Of me dating you. I think he likes you."

I laughed as I thought about the night I accused him of that and he looked like he wanted to die. "No. I assure you. He doesn't. Seriously, Evan, it's not like that. He's just quick to judge. He'll come around."

"If you say so." He leaned in closer. "And what if I did this?" He kissed my cheek, then lingered there. "Would that make him come around faster or slower?"

"Maybe he'd get the point faster," I said.

"Then this would help even more," he whispered, and turned my face toward his. I knew he was going to kiss me, and I froze in panic. What if I did it wrong? He met my eyes, seeming to ask permission, but I still didn't move. He must've taken that as consent because his lips met mine. They felt exceptionally soft, and I wondered if that meant mine were dry. I wasn't sure exactly what to do, which made my stomach drop to my feet. I worried it was obvious. I let him take the lead and it seemed to go okay. I tried to take note of everything he did—the way he moved his head, how he positioned his bottom lip just below mine, the speed of his breath, his hand on my neck—so that next time I'd be better at it.

Gage doing a cannonball into the pool next to us, spraying cold water across the side of my face, pulled me out of the kiss. When Gage came up for air, he said, "It looked like you needed to cool off." He was fully dressed. They must've stopped the game early on my account.

"Yeah, thanks."

"And you guys," Gage yelled back toward the sliding glass door, "didn't jump in on the count of three. You all owe me dinner."

I glanced over my shoulder and saw Braden, Nathan, and Jerom standing by the door. Nathan and Jerom were laughing. Braden walked away.

That night at dinner my brothers all gave their initial impressions of Evan. They were better than I could've hoped for. Braden, who'd stayed to eat with us, scoffed at every nice remark until finally Jerom looked at him and said, "Braden, do you have a problem with Evan?"

"Yes! He's ridiculous. He's everything we told her not to look for in a guy."

"He drinks V8?" Gage asked, mockingly.

Braden grunted. "He's . . . never mind. Apparently he's perfect. Have fun, Charlie."

That night on my cell phone, I got the text: *Fence. Now.*

I thought about ignoring him. He wasn't exactly making it easy to forgive him for his behavior. But maybe I could talk some sense into him. He was my friend and I hated it when we fought.

"Can't you just be happy for me?" I asked at the fence. *I need you to be happy for me,* I thought but didn't say.

"I could if he were right for you."

"You don't even know him."

"*He* doesn't even know *you*." His voice was tight, angry.

I tried to keep my voice light and friendly. "Isn't that what relationships are all about? Getting to know each other?"

"If you were giving him the right information, then yes. But he thinks you're . . . He thinks you're like Amber. He wants an Amber."

"What's wrong with Amber?"

"You're nothing like her."

We were both quiet for a long time. Finally, I sat down, deflated. Braden had proven to me today that half the guys at the game would've asked me out, but now he was saying Evan would be scared away if he knew more about me?

"And you don't think he'd want the real me?"

"No."

I put my forehead to my knees and pulled out handfuls of grass at the edge of the lawn. The pit in my stomach opened wide and wanted to swallow me whole. So if Evan couldn't like me for me, was he implying there was something really wrong with me? "Why are you doing this to me? Why couldn't you just let me figure it out on my own?"

"Because I don't want to see you hurt."

"Unless you're the one hurting me?"

"I'm not trying to, Charlie."

"Maybe I'm more like Amber than you know. Maybe you're the one who doesn't know me." I felt different. Like I was learning more about myself lately. I wasn't just my brothers' little sidekick.

"If you're like her, then maybe I don't want to know you."

An icy pain stabbed in my chest. The grass in my fists

felt cold and rubbery, and even when I opened my hands to release it, several blades stuck to my palms. I wiped them on my pants and stood. "You're being a jerk," I mumbled and walked back into the house.

CHAPTER 27

• • • • • • •

I sat at my desk reading over the list of camp supplies I would need for next week. I had put down the pencil I was using to check off the things I needed to get because I had already gouged a hole through the first item on the list. Where did Braden get the right to judge Evan? And why? He didn't even know him. He didn't even *want* to know him. It wasn't Evan's fault that I was holding back part of myself. It wasn't fair of Braden to say Evan wouldn't accept me when I hadn't given him the chance to.

I pushed myself away from the desk and stood, grateful

for the distraction of work today. If I left now I'd be half an hour early, but I needed to get out of the house.

"Charlie," Linda said with a smile as I walked in. "Your aura looks red today. Are you upset about something?"

She was starting to trip me out with her aura talk, which was usually right on target. "I'm fine. Boys are stupid."

She laughed. "Do you need to talk?"

I held up the backpack of clothes that I needed to change into. I wasn't sure why I still waited until work to change. Everyone at home had now seen me in my nicer clothing. It was tradition, apparently, to change at work. "No, I just need to get my mind off things." I slipped into the back room and quickly changed.

When I came back out, Linda took both my hands in hers. "I'm sure your mom tells you this all the time, but it's always good to hear frequently: we can't let boys define how we feel about ourselves. You have to know who you are before you should let any boy worth anything in."

I tried not to cringe at the mom reference. *My mom doesn't tell me anything,* I wanted to say. But I couldn't. It was too late to come clean. And besides that, I did know who I was. At least I thought I did. I was a girl who grew up without a mom and therefore had no idea how to be a girl. Here I was acting like a huge fake not only to Linda, but to Amber and her friends. When did I become so unsure of myself? When did I ever need to be like someone else? I just needed to get away. Basketball camp would be a good break. I nodded. "Thanks, Linda."

She squeezed my hands and then said, "I have some paperwork to do in the back."

Halfway through my shift, Skye came in holding an ad. "Ooh la la, Charlie. I didn't know you modeled."

I thought she was kidding, when she slid across an ad for the bridal store and there I was, in several shots promoting their makeup line. I noticed two things right away. One, this was not just some cheap paper flyer like Linda had printed out that sat by the register for customers to grab when they came in. It was a nice, shiny color ad a couple of pages long. And two, the pictures weren't extreme close-ups, like Antonia had promised, but my whole body sitting in that chair . . . with my very recognizable face.

I could feel the blood drain as I stared at the ad.

"You okay?" Skye asked.

"I—" I met her eyes. "This isn't . . ." My face felt numb and I wanted to sit down right there behind the register. If my dad saw this, he was going to kill me.

"Where did you get this?" Maybe they hadn't put out the ad yet. It was a local business. Maybe she knew the owner or something. After all, why would Skye be getting ads for a bridal store?

"In the mail."

"The mail? Your mailbox?"

"That would be the one."

"Crap." My adrenaline kicked in and I suddenly felt like running around the city collecting every last ad from every last mailbox. "When? Today?"

"Yes. Just now."

"Can I . . ." I pointed to the ad.

"Yes, keep it. I never go to that store."

"You never go? So do they just send their ad out to everyone in town then?"

She folded the ad in half and handed it to me. "No. I was a bridesmaid once and got put on their mailing list. Now I get their ads all the time."

"Their mailing list? Their mailing list. They have a list. You're on it."

"Are you sure you're okay?"

"I'm fine." I was not on their mailing list. We never got their ads. Nor did anyone I knew. I had never even heard of the store before I had helped out Antonia. My shoulders relaxed.

Skye headed for the back, but she stopped halfway

there and turned around. "Charlie. I didn't mean to offend you the other night at the concert."

"Offend me?"

She used her thumb to point over her shoulder. "About Linda. I didn't mean she'd replace your mother or anything."

"Oh." I suddenly remembered how she told me Linda would soon be as important to me as she was to her. "No. It's okay. I know."

She looked at the floor. "Linda has helped me through a lot. My mom left when I was little. . . ."

I took a slow breath. Now was the time when I told her I hadn't had a mom since I was little either. When I made her feel understood. When I became more understood myself. When I stopped being a fake. I opened my mouth, but she turned without looking up and quickly walked to the back. Who needed to be understood anyway?

To be safe, when I got home, I checked the mail. Happy to see the pile of envelopes inside, meaning I was the first one to check it today, I gathered them in my arms and flipped through the stack. There were a few ads, but not the dreaded one. Now that the shock of it had worn off, my mind spun. They used me in an ad. Without my permission. That was so wrong. Then I remembered the

form the guy had asked me if I'd signed. Oh no. Some
other girl signed a paper giving them permission to use
her image and I filled in for her that day. This was so
unfair. I wondered if she was getting paid for this.

I shut the mailbox and took a few steps toward
Braden's house. I needed someone to talk to and his was
the first face that flashed through my mind. Halfway to
his door, I stopped with a sigh. He was still mad at me,
and I was still mad at him for how big of a baby he had
been about Evan. And for how mean he had been to me
because of it.

I pulled out my phone and called Amber.

"What a coincidence. I just got off the phone with
Braden."

My head whipped over to Braden's house as if he'd be
standing there, hanging up the phone. The porch was,
of course, empty. I gave it a dirty look and walked up
to my front door, entering the house. "Really? How's
Braden?" I didn't mean to say his name with a hint of
sarcasm; it just came out that way.

"He's good. He told me you were going to some sort
of basketball camp next week."

"Yes. I am."

"I didn't know you played basketball."

I took a breath. "I do. And soccer."

"Cool. But too bad you're going to be gone because

I'm having a party next week. I wish you could come."

Cool? That's how simple it was to be myself? I just had to tell her? I felt stupid. "Yeah. I'm going to be gone. But we always do an end-of-the-summer thing here at my house after I get back. You should come."

"Of course. Sounds fun."

I walked up the stairs, my feet telling me I was still upset about the ad by how loud they sounded on each step. "So hey, did you happen to see the ad the bridal store put out today?"

"No. Why?"

"I'm in it." I realized I said that sentence really loudly and looked around to make sure nobody had heard me. The coast was clear, so I went into my room and shut my door.

"What? I didn't know you modeled."

I resisted rolling my eyes and said, "I don't. It's images for their new makeup line. I was in there that day helping out Antonia. I guess the girl that should've been there signed a form. I claimed I was her because they were being all weird about parental permission that day. Now I know why."

"Oh, crap. That sucks."

"Exactly. What should I do?"

"Unfortunately, it sounds like you . . . well, *she* . . . kind of signed over creative rights to your image. I guess

if you got a lawyer involved you might be able to challenge it. But you lied about it, so I don't think you'll have
much recourse there. Are you in big trouble?"

"Are you kidding me? My dad hasn't seen it, and he
won't if I can help it."

"It's just a local ad, Charlie. It could be worse."

I sank onto my bed, feeling defeated. "I know." This
was my payback for all the lies I'd told lately.

"Try not to let it get to you. It's something that people
throw in their recycle bins after barely looking at."

"You're right. I'm glad I'm leaving for a week. Hopefully it will get my mind off everything." And there
were so many things that "everything" meant.

CHAPTER 28

• • • • • • •

grabbed my duffel bag and slung it over my shoulder, picked up my pillow, and headed for the stairs.

"Dad, we need to leave in fifteen minutes," I called down the hall, then took the stairs two at a time and dropped my stuff by the front door. In the kitchen, I grabbed a bowl and poured myself some cereal. The doorbell rang, and since I was the only one up and ready for the day, I went to answer it. "Ready" was a relative term. I had woken up, showered, thrown my hair in a ponytail, and pulled on some sweats. So when I opened the door and saw Evan standing there, I tried to resist the urge to shove my pillow in front of my face. He'd never seen me without makeup. I pursed my lips together. No. This was good. This was how I normally looked, and this would prove he didn't care.

"Hi," he said with a smile. "I didn't want you to leave for a week without saying good-bye in person."

"Oh. Great. Come in." I stood aside. "I was just about to eat some breakfast. Do you want anything?"

"No. Already ate. But don't let me stop you."

As I poured the milk on my cereal, I felt Evan staring. I looked up with a questioning eyebrow raise.

"You look different in the morning," he said.

I couldn't tell if it was a good different or a bad different. "I haven't put my makeup on," I said. *Because I usually don't unless I'm going out,* I should've added.

"Right." He cleared his throat. "So, is this a girls' camp or is it coed?"

"It's coed. But we each have our own dorms, of course." I took a bite of my cereal.

"That's cool. I was just thinking . . . before you left . . . that maybe we should define what we . . ." The back door swung open and Braden stepped inside, his eyes locking with mine. I didn't know if he even saw Evan sitting on the barstool. Braden looked like crap. His hair was a mess, his eyes looked more green than brown today, rimmed with red, like he hadn't slept for days. His T-shirt was wrinkled, and he wore a pair of athletic shorts and flip-flops. Seeing him like that made my heart ache. I wanted to tell him I was sorry for calling him a jerk. There was so much I wanted to say, but I couldn't, not with an audience.

"I'm sorry for the other night. I don't want to leave things like this," he said, without warming up to it. "Truce?"

I looked at Evan, then back at Braden. Braden finally noticed Evan and his expression went dark.

"Hey, man," Evan said.

Braden just nodded, then turned his attention back to me. "Have fun at camp." He backed out the door before I could stop him. I thought about going after him, talking things through. I hated how things were between us too, but as I took a step toward the door, my dad walked into the kitchen.

"Almost ready, Charlie?"

"Yeah."

"Oh, hello, Evan."

Evan stood. "Hi."

I took a couple of spoonfuls of my Cheerios and put the bowl in the sink. "I'm ready. I'll be right out."

He left the kitchen and I gave Evan an apologetic shoulder shrug. I wasn't that sorry, though. I didn't want him to finish the conversation he was trying to start before Braden walked in. I didn't want to define our relationship before I left. I needed the time away to think about our relationship.

"When you get home, I want to take you out," Evan said, coming around the counter and giving me a hug.

"Sounds good." I started to pull away, but then realized he wanted a kiss, too, so I stepped forward again and right onto his foot. "Oh, sorry." I looked down, but apparently he was still going in for the kiss, because we bumped heads. "I'm not doing well this morning."

He slid his hand onto the back of my neck.

"Oh," I said. "Third time's a charm?" I leaned forward and our lips finally met. Knowing my dad was waiting in the car—and with the look that had been on Braden's face moments ago flashing through my mind—I pulled away faster than I might have otherwise. "Thanks."

He smiled. "Have fun." He squeezed my hand, then held on to it as we walked toward the front door. My dad must've gotten my stuff, because it wasn't there anymore.

"Charlie!" A loud cry echoed from upstairs, then what sounded like a stampede came rushing down. Gage wrapped me in a hug. "Be a good girl. Don't work so hard that you barf like you did last year."

"Your words of wisdom are invaluable."

"You barfed last year?" Evan said.

Gage pulled back. "Oh, hey, Evan."

"Hi . . ."

"Gage."

Evan pointed. "Right. Still learning."

"We should hang out while Charlie's gone."

"Yeah . . . sure."

I bit my lip, not sure how I felt about that. I wanted my brothers to get to know Evan. I liked Evan. But I was feeling unsettled, like I still needed to figure out my feelings. I squeezed Gage's hand, went up on my tiptoes, and whispered, "Take Braden out today, okay?" He nodded against my cheek. I backed toward the car. "Well, I'll see you guys later."

I climbed in the car and sank against the seat with a loud sigh.

"Boy troubles?" my dad asked.

I rubbed my hands on my thighs. Could I really talk to my dad about this? It would probably make him uncomfortable. I'd come back from camp and he'd have new advice from his coworker Carol, who was starting to seem a little nosy to me. "I don't know. This is all so new to me that I don't even know what 'boy troubles' means."

He laughed. "Don't think too hard. And you don't have to jump into a relationship with the first boy who looks at you nice, Charlie. If you don't like him, there's nothing wrong with that."

"What makes you think I don't like him?"

"The look of terror on your face when I walked into the kitchen a minute ago."

I started to nod, but then remembered that look wasn't for Evan. My dad walked into the kitchen right after Braden had walked out. "I don't know how I feel." And that was the truth. I hoped camp would help me sort things out.

CHAPTER 29

• • • • • • •

Camp took place at a little private college on the coast, three hours south of us. The first two days at camp, I shut everyone and everything out, even my friends I hadn't seen since last summer. I got in the zone, focusing only on the game. It felt good to let my body take over and my mind think only about basketball.

"Keep playing like that, Charlie, and you're going to have your pick of colleges," one of the coaches said as I threw my ball into the bin to leave the gym for the night.

"Thanks, coach."

I left the gym and breathed in the coastal air. I didn't

usually run on the beach. I wasn't sure why. Our house was only about ten miles inland. I hadn't wanted to tie up the car for my daily run. But the ocean helped me sink even farther into my brainless routine. Its repetitive rhythm and steadiness lent to my complete shutout of the world around me. So I headed to the beach for a pre-dinner run. It was freeing not to have restrictions on what time of day I could run. Some other kids from camp had the same idea, and I fell in step with a group of guys who I knew from last summer.

We all greeted each other but didn't disrupt our run with talking. This was what I liked about camp—a lot of focused people coming together. This was me. Already this week had redirected me, reminded me about what I loved. The game. The competition. So did that mean there was no place in my life for other things?

No. I just had to bring myself to the game and make sure everyone still wanted to be part of my life. Braden was right, as hard as it was to admit: Evan didn't know all of who I was. But he was wrong about the other part— that Evan wouldn't like me if he did. I thought he would. I smiled and picked up my pace.

With my hair still wet from my shower, I headed for my dorm room, ready to sleep hard tonight. I opened the door. Susie looked up from where she lay on her bed, staring at her phone. She'd been my roommate for the last two years.

"Hey, Charlie."

Our schedules had been off this year because we were on different teams, so this was the first chance I'd really gotten to talk to her. I kicked off my flip-flops and threw my duffel bag into the corner. "Hi."

"You're killing it out there this year. I need whatever coach you've been using."

I smiled. "It's called the trying-to-sort-out-boys program."

She sat up on her bed and tossed her phone onto the nightstand. "I'm listening."

I groaned. "There's nothing to tell. One boy is driving me crazy and another boy might not be the One." I sank onto my bed with another groan.

"Tell me about him."

"Which one?"

She shrugged. "Both."

"Evan. He's cute and nice and fun."

"But . . ."

I laughed. "But maybe I haven't been completely myself around him."

"Why?"

"I don't know. I thought he wouldn't like me."

"Well, that's no good."

"I know."

"And what about the other boy? Is he a contender in the race for your heart too?"

"I don't think there's really a race. But no, he's not. He's my neighbor and apparently thinks he's my boss. He's mad at me for dating Evan. He doesn't like him."

"Braden?"

I whipped my head toward her.

"This is our third summer together, Charlie. I do know things."

"Right. And yes, Braden."

"What doesn't he like about him?"

"He thinks he's . . ." I tried to think of the word Braden used to describe Evan. "Ridiculous."

"Why?"

"I don't know. Because he wears loafers or something. No good reason."

She smiled knowingly. "So Braden is jealous. You didn't tell me Braden liked you."

"No. He doesn't."

"What makes you think he doesn't like you?"

I rolled onto my side, hugging my pillow to my chest. "He told me."

"Ouch."

"No. It's not like that. I don't like Braden. Well, okay, I was crushing on him for a while, but we're friends. We can't like each other like that. It was more embarrassing than hurtful," I said, remembering the humiliation that night by the fence.

"Does he like another girl?"

"No. Well, actually, yes. One I introduced him to."

"What does she have that you don't?"

I gave a single laugh. "Femininity."

She threw a wadded-up sock at me. "Who wants that?"

"Apparently guys."

Susie laughed. "So I hear." She rolled onto her back. "If he doesn't want you for you, then he's not worth it."

Hadn't Braden said those exact same words to me when referring to Evan? I laughed. "Susie. You're not hearing me. I don't want Braden . . . anymore. Our friendship is more important to me." But did we even have that anymore? My heart sank with the thought that maybe I had ruined that. Or he did.

"So then you're going to try with Evan?"

"I don't know. He's fine. He just knows the other me, not the real me."

She raised one eyebrow. "Other you?"

"Yes, I have a bit of a split personality, apparently. Long story."

"We have all night."

I filled her in on my side job and why I had to get it. On how I met Evan, and Braden's reaction to him.

"Wait, so if Braden hates his guts and Evan really is a nice guy, don't you think that means Braden is jealous?"

"No, Braden thinks I'm being fake around Evan."

"And you are?"

"Sometimes."

"But why would Braden care so much unless he cared? You know what I mean?"

"He cares. Just not like that." I rearranged my pillow and adjusted my position. "I'm just glad I'm here. I needed a break from both of them."

"Breaks are good. Maybe the time away will help clarify things."

That's exactly what I hoped for. "You got the light?" I asked.

"You're closer."

"Am not."

She picked up a stuffed basketball next to her and threw it across the room at the light panel, plunging us into darkness. "Nice shot," I said.

"Thanks."

Susie snored. I knew this because I could not sleep. She needed one of those machines with the straps. I'd have to tell Braden.

It was only eleven, but I should've been exhausted. My brain wouldn't shut off. I told Susie that I hoped this week would help me clarify things, but I realized I wasn't trying to clarify anything. I was trying to shut everything out. That was why I was working so hard. Physical exertion made me forget; the adrenaline, the high of the competition helped me block out everything else.

What I really needed right now was to sit by the fence and talk about my problems with Braden. I wanted to hear the timbre of his voice as he responded to me. He had a very soothing voice. And he always knew just what to say . . . except he seemed to be saying all the wrong things lately and making me mad. Nobody could make me as mad as he could. It was probably because he knew me so well that he knew what bothered me the most.

I could picture his face perfectly—hazel eyes, floppy auburn hair, a very light dusting of freckles. The way his cheeks turned red when he worked too hard. Like that night he ran behind me for five miles when we were fighting, just so I wouldn't run alone. His cheeks had been so red that night.

I moved to my side and readjusted my blankets. I closed my eyes, but all I could see was his face with his lopsided smile. That was my favorite. It was like he was amused but didn't want to admit it. He gave me that look a lot. Like the time he beat me in one-on-one basketball. I liked that he didn't let me win, but I was so mad that he won. He found that so amusing.

I wasn't amused right now. Right now I was still hurt that Braden didn't think Evan could like me for me. Why did I care what Braden thought anyway? It didn't matter. My brothers seemed to think Evan was nice. That was enough.

Only it wasn't.

Why wasn't it?

I growled and moved onto my back, staring at the shadows on the ceiling, hoping they could tell me the answer to that question. The only thing I saw on the ceiling was Braden's face.

My heart gave a jolt and I sat up. Crap.

I knew why I cared. Why this mattered so much. Why his opinion was the only thing that mattered.

I was more than just crushing on him. I loved Braden.

CHAPTER 30

• • • • • • •

I stared at my phone. I knew I should call Braden. The way he'd looked when I left haunted me. He looked tormented. I wished I didn't care so much. No. I wished he cared more. No. That was wrong too. It was obvious he cared. I wished he cared differently.

I pushed my fists to my eyes and willed the sting to go away. How did I not know that I loved Braden? I mean, I knew I was reacting to him differently. But I hadn't realized just how deep the feelings went. How long had I loved him? That's why it hurt so badly out at the fence when he told me he didn't like me—because I'd wanted him to. Badly. I had just thought I was humiliated, but I was disappointed. If my mom were still alive, would I call her about something like this? Would we have been close? I heard people say all the time that they hated their moms. I wondered if I would've taken her for granted if I'd had her all this time. I certainly couldn't call my dad. He'd have no idea what to say. He'd probably tell me not to ruin my friendship with Braden by talking about it. He'd be right. This was an impossible situation. I needed Braden in my life. I couldn't lose him by telling him I loved him.

My phone chimed and my heart jumped. I looked at the message. It was from Gage. I tried not to be too disappointed as I read it.

If you meet a guy named Fredrick, tell him he still owes me two dollars. Miss you.

I texted back: *You want me to tell Fredrick he owes you two dollars and that you miss him?*

Ha ha.

I smiled. *Miss you too.* I stared at my phone, waited for him to say more. He didn't. It was maddeningly silent for two minutes. Finally, I typed: *Have you been hanging out with Braden?*

Yeah.

And?

And what?

My brother was so dense sometimes. I just wanted to know if Braden was okay. But now that I'd admitted to myself that I was in love with him, it felt like everyone would see that. Maybe everyone had seen it. Did everyone but me know I was in love with Braden?

I sighed. *And nothing. I just wondered if you guys were dying without me.*

Of course we are.

Probably not dying like I was. Man, I needed to run twice as far tomorrow. *Night, Gage.*

Night, Charles Barkley.

I hadn't worn makeup in eight days. It felt nice. I didn't have to scrub my eyes every night with face wash. It also felt good to be competitive again. Before coming to camp, I hadn't played a pickup game with my brothers in over a week. I missed it.

Susie held up a sock. "Is this yours?"

"Oh. Yes."

She threw it to me and I shoved it in my duffel bag, getting everything ready to leave first thing in the morning.

"You'll have to Facebook me so you can tell me all about how your boy issues turned out."

I laughed. "Yeah, I'm curious to see myself." I liked Susie. If she lived closer to me, we would be better friends. I knew I was missing that kind of friendship in my life. Maybe I could have it with Amber one day. . . . I just had to be more honest with her. I needed to be honest with Linda, too. She brought something into my life that I'd never had before. She could read my emotions like the men around me never could. I needed someone to understand me. To help me understand myself. But first I had to come clean. The huge lie I'd told her made it hard to get too close.

But the one truth that stood above the other ones I'd take away from camp was that I was in love with Braden Lewis. I loved him so much it hurt. It hurt because I knew he couldn't love me back the way I needed him to. And I was going to have to learn to live with that, because I couldn't lose him. I would have to be happy with whatever part of Braden I could have.

There was a pounding on the window and Susie looked over at me. I shrugged and cranked it open.

"Charlie. It's the last night. You said it was prank night," came a whisper from the beach below.

Susie groaned. "We're too tired."

"Don't be babies," someone else called.

My competitive nature flared up. "We'll be out in a minute." I shut the window.

"For real?" Susie asked me, rolling onto her side.

I smiled a wicked smile. "It's tradition."

"Fine. What are we doing this year?"

"Filling Fredrick's dorm room with basketballs. He owes my brother two dollars. I think this will be better than collecting money."

She laughed. "Well, why didn't you say that to begin with?"

"I just thought of it."

"How do we get the keys to the gym?"

"We'll figure it out."

CHAPTER 31

• • • • • • •

I let out a happy sigh as Jerom pulled in to our driveway. Camp was fun, but it was so nice to be home. I wanted to check on Braden, make sure he was okay. I should've called him while I was gone. That's what a good friend would've done. I felt bad that I was too busy licking my wounds to be a good friend.

Jerom parked the car in the garage and we went in through the kitchen. Nathan sat at the counter with a girl I'd never met before.

"You're home, Charlie."

"I'm home."

Jerom brushed by me with my bag. "I'll put this in your room."

"Thanks. You're the best."

"I know."

I rolled my eyes, but he didn't see my display because he was already out of the kitchen. I turned back toward the stranger sitting next to Nathan. "I don't know you."

She smiled. She was cute. A small Asian girl with long black hair and a big smile.

Nathan stood and gave me a hug. "This is Lauren. And Lauren, this is my sister, Charlie."

"Lauren? As in, disc golf Lauren?"

Nathan nodded. "Yes. This is the one we returned the Frisbee to."

"Wow. You don't look big *or* burly," I told her. Or, as Braden had put it, tall and strong. And from the way my brother smiled at her, I could tell he was into her. My heart sank a little. Not because I didn't want Nathan to like her, but because I didn't think Braden would ever look at me that way.

"Excuse me?"

"Inside joke. Sorry. Good to meet you, but I just got home from camp and—"

"You need a shower," Nathan interrupted.

I punched his arm. "Thanks a lot. I was going to say nap. We were up all night pranking. But shower first, I guess."

I left him and Frisbee Girl in the kitchen and walked through the door to the living room. I wanted to turn around and walk back out again. Amber sat on the couch, sandwiched between Braden and Gage as they watched television. Braden looked good. Happy, even. His eyes were clear. His hair was perfectly messy.

My heart gave an excited flutter at seeing him and I had to force it to calm down, remind it who was sitting closer than necessary right next to him. Gage jumped up the second he saw me and wrapped me in a hug.

"I missed you, Charles Barkley."

I closed my eyes, trying to ignore the stinging there. "Missed you, too."

"You stink."

I smacked his back. "Thanks. Oh, I collected your two dollars from Fredrick . . . sort of."

"Tell."

"He was asleep last night and we filled his dorm floor with basketballs. It was awesome." I tried to make my voice sound light and happy as I told him the story. Like I'd had all the fun in the world while I was gone.

It seemed to work, because Gage laughed. "You are the man . . . well, the she-man."

"Thanks," I mumbled. I waved to Amber and Braden. "Hi. I've been told I need a shower . . . twice now . . . but are you hanging out for a while?"

They both said, "Yes," then looked at each other and

laughed. My stomach clenched. I had only been gone for a week, but suddenly between Nathan's new girl and now Braden, it felt like I'd missed out on months of developments. Missed out on my chance. I shouldn't have left. Braden needed me and I had walked away. Maybe Amber helped him out of his funk.

"Okay. I'll be right back."

In the shower, the water ran down my face. My stomach hurt and my eyes hurt and my head throbbed. A weird lump had formed in my throat, and I wondered if I was getting sick. Then a sob escaped. A sob that made my heart twist and my insides want to come out. I leaned my forehead against the tile as another one came, followed by tears. It hurt to cry. I didn't like it. But I couldn't stop. What was my problem? It wasn't like I'd lost anything. I knew Braden didn't like me the way I finally admitted to liking him. But I hadn't expected to have it thrown in my face so soon upon returning.

I turned off the shower, toweled dry, and dressed. I crept across the hall to my dad's room and knocked. Jerom had told me my dad was working the late shift tonight, so I figured he'd be sleeping. I didn't want to wake him, but I needed someone to talk to. He didn't answer so I let myself in. His bed was made and empty.

I sank onto it and pulled his pillow against my chest.

My hand bumped something hard. A book. I stared at the title for a long time: *How to Raise a Teenage Girl.* He needed a book on how to raise me? He must've thought I was turning out wrong. The pages of the book were dog-eared and worn, well used. And they obviously hadn't helped. I still hadn't turned out right. The stupid girl on the cover looked more normal than me. My eyes collided with the author's name on the bottom of the cover: Carol Franks. This was Carol? This was who had given him advice about me for the last several years?

I needed my mom. More tears tried to gag me. It was painful to cry, but it seemed to loosen something in my chest. I pushed the book back under the pillow and checked my face in the mirror to make sure no evidence of my weakness showed. I stared at my reflection. This was me. Hopeless. I made my way back downstairs. Everyone was still in the same position as before on the couch. I glanced at the television.

"What are you guys watching?" It definitely wasn't sports. It looked like some sort of romantic comedy. Did I walk into the twilight zone?

Amber smiled. "Something you'll love. These boys need to let the girls have a pick once in a while, right? And it was my pick today." Her statement implied they'd been hanging out multiple days. "Besides, they lost a bet."

"What bet was that?"

Amber laughed and couldn't stop. Gage joined her. I was beginning to wonder if the bet was who could be the most annoying, because I could see how Amber would easily win that.

"Amber had a party this week," Braden said. "And she has this huge backyard, so we were driving golf balls trying to hit a . . . uh . . . target—"

They all laughed again.

"And she hit it," Braden was finally able to finish.

They probably wanted me to ask what the target was, but that would just make them laugh harder. And I would feel even less a part of this inside joke. Knowing my brothers, the target was probably someone's butt or someone's car. So instead I said, "Really? She beat Gage?"

"I did!" Amber yelled, raising both arms in the air.

"And no one received a concussion as a result or anything, right?"

Gage let out a bursting laugh. "There were helmets."

Braden scooted closer to Amber and patted the couch cushion beside him. I took a deep breath. Yes. I needed to go sit by him. To show him that we could be friends like we always were. A good friend who wouldn't notice that he scooted closer to Amber to make room for me, instead of farther away from her. Not only would a good

friend not notice that, but she would be happy that he'd
found such a nice, fun girl like Amber.

I dug my nails into my palm and walked closer. He
looked up and I noticed his left eye was rimmed with
black. I gasped. "What happened?"

He smiled.

"I guess the helmet didn't help?" I asked, realizing
he probably took a turn as one of the golf ball targets.
Sometimes they were the biggest idiots.

I sat next to him. His familiar scent washed over me
and threatened to bring tears back to my eyes. I scooted
as far to edge of the couch as possible, practically hugging the armrest. My effort only provided an inch of
space between our bodies. Not nearly enough.

He brushed his arm against mine. "We good?" he
asked.

I bit my lip and nodded.

"Good, because I was wrong about Evan. I was being
a judgmental jerk."

No, I wanted to yell. *You weren't. And now if you like
him that means you weren't really being jealous at all.*

"He's actually pretty cool," he said when I didn't
respond.

"Really cool," Amber butted in. "He's been hanging out with us this week. Did you know Evan has a
boat? You should see these pictures he has of himself

wakeboarding. He's even been in a tournament."

Were Braden and I really making up in front of Amber? I felt cheated. I wanted a fence make-up, where we had the moon and the stars and nobody else but the two of us. Where we got to tell each other how stupid we'd been and what great friends we were. "Cool," was all I could manage.

"You okay?" he asked.

I nodded again.

"I missed you."

I focused really hard on the television, determined not to cry. I wished the sappy movie playing out in front of me was a baseball game. I gasped. "We're not missing the A's for this are we?"

Braden growled.

"We're recording the game," Amber said. "A bet is a bet."

Since when would Braden let a bet supersede a game? I would not let this bother me. I gripped the armrest harder. One of his hands went to my knee and he started to write letters out with his finger. I tried to concentrate, but each letter sent tingles up my leg. I had no idea what he was spelling. I shrugged and he started over. This time I concentrated harder. D-O-N-T-B-E-M-A-D-I-W-A-N-T-T-O-W-A-T-C-H-T-H-E-G-A-M-E-T-O-O.

I took his hand and turned it palm up on my knee, then spelled out Y-O-U-S-U-C-K.

He laughed.

The girl in the movie was giving some sort of speech to her best friend about why she needed to fight for the guy. I had no idea what she was saying, though, because Braden's hand remained on my knee, palm up, long after I finished my message to him. It was the only part of him that touched me, and my entire knee burned. It distracted me from any coherent thought. Why did he leave it there? Shouldn't he move it? Was he just into the movie and didn't realize where his hand was? We'd sat next to each other on the couch for years. He was probably just so comfortable with me that he didn't even think twice about his hand on my knee. And yet here I was getting all obsessed about it—reading way more into it than was necessary. It was a hand. It was a knee. They happened to be touching. Big deal.

"Have you called Evan yet?" Amber asked. "We should invite him over. Let's do something fun tonight."

"I have to work tomorrow and I'm super tired," I said. "It's been a long week." I knew I needed to talk to Evan alone before we had a group date of any sort. I had to tell him that I wasn't feeling it. My heart wasn't in it. When my heart could let go of Braden, maybe I'd be more open to something with someone else. But I was in no place to date anyone right now.

"Well, we still have time before school starts. Maybe he can take us out on the boat next week."

"It'll have to be before the big end-of-the-summer party." Braden squeezed my knee, sending a zap of electricity through my body, and then moved his hand back to his own lap. I must've gasped at the feeling, because he looked at me with a furrowed brow.

It's nothing, Braden, just every time you touch me, my body reacts, that's all. I stood. "Good to see everyone, but I'm going to take a nap now." And get away from Braden.

Braden grabbed my arm and pulled me back down next to him. "No. We haven't seen you in a week. You have to stay down here."

"I'm tired."

"Go to sleep then."

"I was trying to."

"No. Right here."

"Yeah," Gage piped in. "Don't leave us."

"Oh my gosh, you guys turned into babies when I left. Fine. I'll stay."

Braden reached behind him and retrieved one of the throw pillows. I positioned it on the arm of the couch and lay down. In the past, I would've thrown my legs over his, but I couldn't. It seemed so obvious now. He'd know if I did that.

He, obviously not worried about appearances, dragged my legs onto his lap. "See, nice and comfortable."

I hoped he couldn't feel the change in my breathing in response to his action. I wasn't sure I could sleep at all now.

CHAPTER 32

• • • • • • •

Rain beat against the windows and the wind howled. I knew it was a dream, I knew exactly what dream it was, and yet I couldn't wake up. My mind was paralyzed as it waited for the final element to come into play—my mom. Only this time, she didn't show up in my room like she always did. Instead, I was transported into her car. In the backseat as it careened along the road, seeming to blow back and forth with the wind.

Outside was only blackness. I couldn't see the scenery, only red rain pounding the windows. I didn't want to be in the car. For the first time, I noticed my mom's face was streaked with tears. She was crying. Sobbing.

I couldn't feel the car tumbling, but I saw the world spin—my mom's arms fly in the air, glass fan out in a pattern around us, its sharp edges sparkling—and then everything was still. The rain was gone, the glass was gone, and all I could see in between the front seats was my mom's pale arm, limp and red with blood. I screamed.

My eyes popped open to silence, my jaws clamped together. It took me three counts to remember where I was. Braden still sat there, trapped by my legs. But everyone else was gone. Laughter came from the kitchen and I realized Gage and Amber were in there. I took several deep breaths to try to even out my breathing.

It wasn't until Braden squeezed my hand that I became aware he was holding it. I quickly let go and sat back, wiping the sweat from my face.

"Talk to me," Braden said. "Were you having a nightmare?"

"Yes."

"About your mom?"

"Yes." I hugged my knees to my chest and stared at the space on the cushion between us. "There's not much to talk about. It was just a dream." And I was sure that my mom was crying in it this time because of how much I had cried today. Dreams were weird like that.

He took several deep breaths. "When you were ten,

you opened your window, popped out the screen, and climbed onto your roof. Do you remember that?"

I thought back, wondering why he was bringing this up. "Yes."

"Were you scared at all, Charlie? Because I remember when we all discovered you after hours of searching the neighborhood, you were just sitting there, acting like it was nothing big."

"I don't remember feeling much of anything. Maybe I was a little scared."

"Do you remember why you climbed out there?"

"No. Why, do you know?"

"Yes."

I finally met his eyes and the look of pity there sent a jolt of fear through me. "Why? Why are you looking at me like that? Why are you telling me this?"

He grabbed my hand and held it tight in his. This made me more afraid. "Do you remember your dad and your brothers wanted to have a talk with you? About your mom?"

"My mom?" I thought back, trying to piece together the fragments of my ten-year-old memory. I remembered running up the stairs to get to my room. I remembered climbing out my window and onto the roof. I didn't remember why, though. My head pounded as I pushed my thoughts. My dad had sat me on the couch and started talking about my mom. I do remember my head got fuzzy and my ears felt like they were filled with cotton. I had needed air. That was why I had climbed out my window. "What was he trying to tell me?"

Braden's voice became soft, his thumb making circles on the back of my hand. "Your dad wanted to tell you what really happened to your mom that night."

"When she got in a car accident?"

He looked at me hard. "You really don't remember what he said? If you don't, Charlie, it's not my place to say. I just thought you remembered and you needed someone to talk to about it. I thought that's why you've been having the nightmares."

A gray-haired man with glasses flashed in my mind. I was sitting in a chair with my feet dangling off. I must've been young. He had me draw pictures. I drew rain and glass. Red rain. I squeezed my eyes shut. The image of a pale, lifeless hand filled the blackness. "Tell me."

"Shh. It's okay." He pulled me against his chest, and that's when I felt the moisture on my cheeks. I wiped it away quickly, embarrassed by its presence.

"You're so strong, Charlie. You'll remember. I'll be here when you do."

Part of me wanted to beg him to tell me. The other part, the part that was still embarrassed by the tears in my eyes, wanted to shut it out and never think of it again. Wanted to get in a car and speed away from my past. His heart beat against my cheek in a steady rhythm. Every beat drew me closer to him. Soon his hand started making lazy circles on my back. This was the definition of torture, I was sure of it—loving someone who only wanted to be your friend.

"I want to know," I finally said. I felt like I could handle anything with him there.

"Then you need to talk to your dad."

"He's working a late shift. I won't see him until after I work tomorrow. Can't you tell me?"

"I can't. It's not my place."

Another loud laugh came from the kitchen, and I felt Braden's gaze shift to the door. I wondered if he wished he were in there with Amber. If he was nervous about Gage spending time with her. The thought was enough to sit me up straight, pushing away from Braden.

"I'm good," I said, wiping my eyes to make sure they were free of any traces of tears. "I think I'm just really tired. It was a long week."

"So you probably don't want to play soccer this afternoon? Your brother organized a game." He was trying to make me feel better. He thought soccer would help. And it normally would've, but right now I wanted to call my dad and find out what everyone seemed to be keeping from me. "I'm sorry. You have a lot to process right now."

I forced a smile. "Stop reading me. It's creepy."

"But you're like a book. I told you, I know more about you than you know about me."

Our eyes met. His reference to our fence chats, thrown out there so blatantly during the middle of the day, made my cheeks go hot for a moment. And what was he trying to say with that statement? That he knew what I discovered at camp? That my feelings for him were plainly written all over my face?

Amber's laugh brought us out of our eye-lock. She poked her head into the room. "Braden, Gage is doing it again. Come beat him up."

More inside jokes that I wasn't part of. I stood abruptly. "I need to sleep more."

Braden grabbed my wrist. "Fence tonight?"

I gave the smallest nod and then went upstairs.

CHAPTER 33

● ● ● ● ● ● ●

I played with the edge of the quilt on my bed. I'd tried to call my dad several times, but he must've been busy, because the call went straight to voice mail. I didn't feel like this was something I could leave in a message.

Braden hadn't said a time to meet out at the fence. It was midnight now. Everyone was asleep. But Braden's room was dark as well. I clutched my cell phone close and lay down, waiting for his text or for my dad to call me back.

The next thing I knew, a ray of sunlight was shining in my eyes. I sat up and looked at the clock on my nightstand. Crap, I was going to be late for my first day back to work. I searched my bed for the cell phone and found it wrapped in the covers. The screen was blank, no missed texts. He must've fallen asleep as well last night. Or maybe he had been out with Amber.

On the way down the hall, I poked my head into my dad's room. He was out cold. I resisted the urge to wake him up, make him talk. But I was already late. It would have to wait a little longer. It had waited years, apparently; what was a few more hours?

"Charlie. Welcome back." Linda gave me a hug. "Did you have fun?"

"It was nice."

"You look like you got some sun."

"Beach running."

"Ah. If only I could be in as good shape as you are."

"What are you talking about, Linda? You could kick my trash any day of the week."

Linda laughed and swatted her hand through the air.

"I'm going to change."

In the back room, I slipped into my work clothes. They felt comfortable now, even normal. Maybe it was my body I was more comfortable with. My body that I'd been trying to hide behind baggy clothes for years. I was bigger than other girls—taller, stronger—but that wasn't a bad thing.

I came back out and didn't see him at first, standing in

the corner. Not until Linda nodded her head to the side. I looked at Evan. He checked the price tag of a necklace on a mannequin.

"Hey, Evan."

He turned and smiled, his eyes lighting up. "You're back and you didn't even call me."

"I was so tired yesterday. Sorry." I looked at Linda and she nodded, seeming to read my mind. "Do you want to talk in the back for a minute?"

"Sure."

I led him to the stockroom. "Do you want something to drink? There's water."

"No. I'm good." He shoved his hands in his pockets.

"We need to talk," we both said at the same time.

He laughed. "Go ahead."

"No, you go first."

"Okay." He looked at the ground then back up at me. I suddenly remembered what he had tried to talk about before I left for basketball camp: our relationship. He opened his mouth.

"I better go first," I blurted out.

He laughed. "Sure."

"I'm . . ." Wow, this was hard. I'd never done this before, and I felt bad. I didn't want to hurt him, but at the same time, I knew I couldn't be with him. My heart just wasn't in it, and that wasn't fair to him. Between the supposedly huge secret I needed to pry out of my dad and my feelings for Braden, I couldn't string Evan along like this. "I'm in a weird place."

He seemed to sense what was happening and his entire demeanor changed. His eyes became guarded. "Are you breaking up with me?" He seemed shocked. Like this had never happened to him before.

"I . . ." Had we been together? "Yes. I'm sorry. I need to figure things out. Maybe in a few months, when I'm in a better place . . ."

A booming voice sounded from the main room and Evan turned around. "What was that?"

"I don't know." I listened and the voice came back, angry. "Oh no. It's my dad."

"Your dad?"

I ran down the hall but paused right before the sales floor, wanting to know what he was upset about before barreling in there.

"She's sixteen years old," he said.

I couldn't hear Linda's response.

"I did not give her permission to do this! You should not have let her."

Nathan must've told him about my makeup sessions. I needed to get out there and smooth things over. Only when I entered the room, still unnoticed by either my dad or Linda, I saw how my dad really found out. He held—and was angrily waving—the ad from the bridal store in Linda's face. Oh no.

And now I could finally hear her. "This is not my ad, sir. You're going to have to ask your daughter about this."

"But she did this makeup stuff for you, too."

"Yes. She got permission from your wife."

I tried to open my mouth to interject, but before I could, my dad spit out, "My wife is dead."

I gasped, and both he and Linda turned toward me.

"Charlie, we are leaving. Now," he growled, then marched out the door.

I could feel Evan over my left shoulder, breathing. He was probably glad he was on his way out of my life after that.

In front of me, Linda just stared. She looked hurt and angry. I guess I wouldn't have to quit now. Linda would ask me to leave.

"I'm so sorry," I said, my voice quieter than I intended.

She looked to the door, where my dad had left. "You'd better go."

I nodded, unable to find any excuse to make this better, and I followed after my dad.

He paced in front of his police car. I headed for the car I'd driven.

"No," he said, and pointed to the passenger side.

"But . . ."

He pointed again, more forcefully, so I climbed in. The police radio was in the middle of a broadcast, and he turned it down and started the car. "We need to talk."

"I'm sorry. She asked me about Mom, and I didn't want to tell another person that she was dead. I didn't want her feeling sorry for me. I wasn't thinking. It was stupid."

He backed out of the parking spot and started to drive.

"I didn't know the bridal store was going to put out that ad. If I'd known, I would've asked you if it was okay."

My dad pulled into a parking lot at the beach, turned off the car, and then stared through the front window at the ocean. He wasn't talking, and that was unnerving. I waited for him to explode like he had in the store, but he just sat there, eerily calm. Probably because I was confessing everything without him having to say a word. And there was something else I needed to confess, something I'd been in denial about, something I'd been running from for years. I was done running. I heard it come out of my mouth and hang in the air before I even thought about how I was going to word it: "I want to know what happened the night Mom died."

CHAPTER 34

• • • • • •

He wasn't expecting that request. I could tell by the way the color drained from his face. "Okay. What exactly do you want to know?"

"What happened that night? There's something more than you're telling me."

"Charlie, I've tried to talk to you about this before. You weren't ready. It nearly broke you."

"I'm ready now." I said it confidently, even though I felt everything but.

"There's no easy way to say this." He raked a hand through his hair as if trying to prove his statement. "Your mother . . ." He hesitated. "She was very sick."

My ears started to buzz and my head felt fuzzy, just like it had when I was ten. I wasn't going to let that stop me this time. "I don't understand."

He took my hand, his grip soft but sure. His eyes went glassy and that terrified me. I held my breath.

"It wasn't an accident."

I squeezed my eyes shut. What that single sentence implied was something I didn't want to accept. "How do you know?"

"She left a note."

Like a tidal wave, everything made sense. My mom was depressed. I knew this. It's why I had no memories of her as a child—she wasn't around. She didn't want to be.

The police radio crackled in my ear and my dad flipped a switch, turning it off. The dashboard of the car pushed against my forehead, and I tried to press against it harder, hoping the pain would rid me of the thoughts.

"Charlie."

I shook my head back and forth.

"Charlie. You knew this. Come here." He pulled me against his chest. "You've known this. Breathe. It's going to be okay."

I nodded, but I wasn't sure it was ever going to be okay again. My mom left me. On purpose.

My dad smelled like . . . my dad—a cross between a musky cologne and cinnamon gum. This was the smell of my entire childhood. He was my childhood. My life. I remembered him at every important event, every unimportant event. All the places she never was.

He shifted a little, his hand moving to wipe at his face. I didn't want to look up and see if that meant he was crying. I couldn't face seeing his pain when mine was already too unbearable. But I didn't have to look up; I heard it in his voice when he said, "And she almost took you with her."

That statement had me sitting up faster than I intended, blood rushing up the back of my head. "I was in the car." I had realized that right away, but I hadn't put the pieces together. No wonder I'd been trying to deny this my whole life. The dreams. The way I could picture that car spinning, glass flying, so perfectly. Her hand lying there limp in front of me. It wasn't just a dream. It was a memory.

"She didn't know," he said quickly. "You snuck into the car. You were supposed to be in bed."

I let out a little breath. At least she didn't try to take me with her. That thought didn't help at all. But it was something, and right now I felt a whole lot of nothing. I was numb.

★ ★ ★

It was a quiet drive back to the shop, where we'd left the other car. My dad kept opening his mouth to say something and then shutting it again. Eventually he spit out, "You have questions. What are they?"

I hadn't thought about questions yet, but I knew I needed to. "Did she see someone? Try to get help?"

"She saw someone regularly. But she was constantly going on and off her medication. She would think she was better. I had you see someone too, right after she died. I had all of you see someone."

Yes, I had memories of the gray-haired man having me draw pictures. "Why didn't you tell me sooner?"

"I tried, Charlie. You weren't ready. You shut down. You climbed on the roof and scared me to death. I decided to wait after that. You were doing so well, I didn't want this to define you."

"I feel stupid. I'm so weak."

"Charlie. No." His hand went to my shoulder. "No, you're not. What child wants to think that about their mom? She was your world."

No. She wasn't. She was barely part of my life. "Jerom, Nathan . . . Gage?"

"They know."

I coughed to try to get rid of the lump in my throat and then put my cheek against the passenger-side window. "I feel stupid." No wonder my dad and brothers thought I was so breakable. Why they protected me so much. "I'm sorry I wasn't another boy."

"What?" We pulled up to the store and he put the car in park.

"I didn't turn out right. I'm broken."

"Oh, Charlie. No."

"I found that book in your room. Carol, your 'coworker.'"

His cheeks went red. "Baby, that's just to help me talk to you about girl things. And I'm obviously not very good at it. I just wanted to do it right. To be what you needed. I know I'm not. I'm not your mom. She would've done it better."

I grabbed his hand in mine so tightly. I wouldn't cry again. "You did it right," I choked. "You did it right."

He took my face in his hands and kissed my forehead. "I must've done something right, because look at the amazing person you turned out to be. Confident, smart, athletic, and beautiful. I love you, kid."

"Love you too."

He brushed at my cheeks. "I need to get back to work. I'm going to call one of your brothers to come get you."

"No. Dad. Please. I need to drive. I need to sit with this whole mom thing alone."

He pulled his brows down low.

"Please. I'll be careful. I won't be long."

He nodded. "I'll send out an APB in an hour if you're not home."

I rolled my eyes, but then realized he was serious. "Or you could just call me." I held up my cell phone. I knew he had one of those tracker things on my phone anyway, so it wasn't like my location would be a secret.

He nodded. He'd send someone for me in an hour. So I'd have to make sure I was faster.

"Oh, and Charlie?" he said as I opened the door.

"Yeah?"

"You're grounded until the party."

I looked at the ad sitting on the console between us, crumpled into a ball. "I know. I'm sorry I lied to you."

He smiled. The first one I'd seen since he picked me up. "We all make mistakes."

I climbed out of his car and headed for mine. I glanced at Linda's store, knowing I should go in and explain, but I couldn't bring myself to do it in that moment. First I had somewhere else to be.

I stared at her headstone. I hadn't visited her grave in over a year, so I thought maybe I'd remembered the wording wrong, but there it was, etched in stone: *Loving Mother.*

Anger surged through me. Those words seemed like the biggest lie in the world to me. If she was so loving, why did she do what she did? She was selfish. I kicked a rock and it ricocheted off her headstone.

I heard the crunch of gravel behind me.

"It hasn't even been thirty minutes," I said, irritated my dad couldn't just give me an hour to think this through.

"He told me not to come yet, but I was worried."

I turned toward Jerom. His face was full of concern.

I wasn't only angry at my mom. I was angry at my brothers, too. They had kept this from me. "I'm fine."

"Really?"

"No. I'm screwed up."

"Charlie." His voice was gruff. "Don't do that. You are not screwed up. You have every right to be upset about this."

"But you think I'm weak. It's why you're so protective of me. You think I'm on the verge of breaking."

"No. You're strong. Too strong, sometimes. You think you need to hold on to this all by yourself." He put his arm around my shoulder and stared at the headstone with me. "Let us be here for you."

"But that's the thing. We're not here for each other, are we? I thought we were the best family in the world, but you guys didn't even tell me."

"Dad tried. We just thought it would be better if we waited."

"Until?"

He sighed, obviously frustrated too. "I don't know.

But, Charlie, this"—he pointed to my mom's headstone— "isn't our family. This is something that happened to our family. Our family was strong before this, and it's still strong. Nothing has changed that."

I read the phrase on her headstone over and over again. *Loving Mother.* "My whole life I thought she would've been my best friend. That she would've taught me all the things I needed to know about being a woman. And in a way, it made me resent Dad a little. That he couldn't do it like she would've. And now I find out that she didn't want to. She didn't want to be my mom. I'm mad at her."

He squeezed my shoulder and his breath hitched. I'd never seen my brother even come close to crying, so it surprised me. "You have every right to be."

"I don't know how to get over it."

"You can only go through it."

Sleep was my friend. I didn't remember the last time I had slept so much. Especially since I hadn't done anything active at all that day. I thought I would have the nightmare about my mom over and over, but I didn't. I didn't dream at all. A fogginess had settled into my head and I wanted to get lost in it.

My dad must've told my brothers to leave me alone, because no one bothered me for hours. A strip of sunlight had traveled up my body through the day and had finally found its way to my face. All I had to do was shut my curtains all the way to get rid of it, but I couldn't find the energy to get up. I was so tired. Instead, I just pulled my pillow over my head.

A knock sounded at my door. I didn't respond. If it were Gage, he'd just walk in. The door creaked open.

"What?" I asked, my voice muffled from the pillow. I wondered if they were all going to take turns trying to fix me.

"Hey." It was Braden.

I was glad my head was under the pillow, because my cheeks colored at his presence. I waited to get it under control, then moved the pillow. "Hi."

He eased all the way into my room. "What happened the other night?"

The other night? I searched my memory for what he might be referring to and remembered we were supposed to meet by the fence. "I fell asleep. Sorry." I probably didn't sound as sorry as I should have, because I was too busy feeling sorry for myself.

He held a soccer ball and started bouncing it back and forth between his knees. "Wanna play?"

He was trying to cheer me up, and although I found it really sweet, I didn't feel like hanging out with Braden right then. It would just be one more reminder of something else I couldn't have and how much my life sucked right now. "Not really. But tell everyone hi for me."

"Well, that would be hard since 'everyone' won't be there. It's just me."

Even worse. "Gage is here, I think. He'd probably be up for it."

He kneed the ball in a high arc and it landed on the end of my bed. "Gage isn't here, and I want you."

I couldn't stop my cheeks from blushing this time. He needed to watch his phrasing. He didn't seem to notice, because he added, "Come on. Please." He went to my closet and pulled out my shoes.

"I'm fine, Braden. I don't need cheering up. I promise."

He sat on the bed next to me, pushing my hair into my face. "Why would you need cheering up? Did something happen?"

He hadn't heard? I smacked his hands away and pushed my hair back. "Nothing I want to rehash right now."

"Well, see, I'm not here to cheer you up. I'm here for completely selfish reasons." He held out his hand and gave me puppy-dog eyes. "Don't make me beg."

I kind of wanted to see him beg. I stared at his hand. He kept it steady, hovering in the air between us. I took it.

CHAPTER 35

• • • • • • •

I couldn't decide if Braden had heard about what happened or not, but either way, he had to know that running up a field, kicking a soccer ball, could get my mind off anything. Well, almost anything. It seemed that kicking a ball alongside Braden could not get my mind off him. As we ran, I shoved him and stole the ball.

"Foul," he said with a laugh.

"If you can catch me, I'll give you that foul."

I dribbled the ball faster, toward the net. I could feel him getting closer. Just as I came to the goal, he caught up and wrapped one arm around my waist, dragging me to a halt. Then he spun me away from the ball, let go, and took the ball back. I jumped onto his back.

"Give it up, Lewis."

"You think this is going to keep me from scoring?" He gripped my thighs with his hands, keeping me from jumping off, and continued to dribble the ball.

"Let me down."

"You're the one who jumped up there."

"Don't make me bite you." I opened my mouth and pressed my teeth lightly against his neck.

He slowed to a stop. "You wouldn't dare, cheater."

"I totally would." My words came out slurred against his neck, and I added a little more pressure to my bite. I shouldn't have started this game; it was making my heart race, feeling his skin against my lips, tasting salt.

"Charles," he warned in a low voice.

I laughed. "You just have to let go of my legs."

He let go, and I gave him a playful bite anyway and jumped down, ready to take off after the ball. But he immediately grabbed me and pulled me against him. "You brat."

I laughed. "You're going down." I used one of my legs to sweep his. He stumbled, but didn't let go of me like I thought he would, and we both fell to the ground. He rolled so I was pinned beneath one of his hips and his right arm.

"You shouldn't be able to knock me down so easily. You're amazingly strong, you know that? It's awesome."

I froze, my entire body on fire. I knew if I moved an inch, it would only increase the sensation running through me from his points of contact on me.

"What's wrong?" he asked, suddenly serious. "Did I hurt you?"

"No, just let me up."

At first he looked confused, then a slow smile spread across his lips. "Why?"

"You won. Just let me up."

"I won? You just conceded? Has that ever happened in the history of time?"

"Yes. You won. Braden. Please." I was out of breath and my voice sounded tight.

"But I owe you one bite." He lowered his head to my neck. My heart beat against my ribs. "It's only fair."

Yes, this was the definition of torture. If he knew what this was doing to me, he couldn't possibly continue.

His teeth brushed lightly against my skin and his breath warmed my neck. My fingers dug into his shoulders.

"Just get it over with," I breathed.

He let out a low, breathy chuckle and then applied slightly more pressure to his bite. I barely contained the moan in the back of my throat, but I couldn't keep my eyes from closing.

He lifted his head. "I need to tell you something."

My eyes flew open and met his.

My guard immediately went back up. He was going to tell me about my mom. Little did he know, I had already heard. I wondered if it would've been better if Braden had been the one to tell me at the fence that night. Would it have been less devastating? Probably not. Either way, it was too late now, and I really didn't feel like talking about it. "I already know."

"You do?"

"Yes. My dad told me."

"Your *dad*?"

"Yes."

"Gage," he growled, then rolled onto his back, finally freeing me. "Does he want to kill me?"

My whole body felt cold without him near me. "No. Why would he? It's not your fault."

"True, but that doesn't mean he'd want me to tell you."

"I thought you weren't going to tell me. That it wasn't your place." My eyes started to sting, and I just wanted to stand up and kick the ball again.

He propped himself up on his elbow. "Wait. What are you talking about?"

"What are *you* talking about?"

"You first."

"I know about my mom."

He took a quick breath and sat up to his knees. Concern shaped his brow. "Your dad told you about your mom . . . about how she . . ."

"Yes." I dragged the back of my hand along my cheek and shivered.

He stretched himself out beside me again and pulled me close. "Why didn't you tell me?"

"I thought you knew. And I didn't want to think about it."

"I'm sorry. Do you want to go home?"

I shook my head and buried my face in his chest. I didn't want to go anywhere. "So that's not what you were going to tell me?"

"No. I mean that's what I wanted to tell you that night by the fence before I realized it wasn't my place to tell you. Maybe I should've told you then. Maybe I should've told you years ago. I'm sorry."

"It's not your fault. You're the one who made me confront my dad." I pulled back so I could look in his eyes. "So what, then? What were you going to tell me today?"

"The timing is wrong now. I'll tell you later."

"No. Please. I want to know now. I'm tired of secrets."

He stared at me for a long time, as if trying to read my sincerity. His breath touched my lips. It took everything in me not to close the distance between us. When his lips brushed against mine, I let out an involuntary gasp. Had I done that?

"Am I reading you wrong?" he asked.

I shook my head no. I couldn't find my voice, couldn't dare to believe this meant what I thought it meant.

He let out a slow breath of air that smelled so familiar. "I was going to tell you that."

"You were going to tell me that you wanted to kiss me?"

He nodded. "Is this going to change everything?"

"I sure hope so."

He smiled and his gaze went from my eyes, to my mouth then up to my hair. He tucked a piece behind my ear. "You're so beautiful."

My cheeks heated. "Aren't we supposed to do this at the fence?"

"No. I don't want this to be in our alternate reality. I want this to be in our real one." He met my lips with his. My heart felt like it had just been put through sprints; it raced to life. I grabbed his shoulders and pulled him closer. Against my lips he added, "But we can do this again tonight at the fence if you want."

I smiled. "Wait. What about Amber?"

"What about her?"

"I thought you and she . . ."

He pulled back, his eyes going wide. "What? No! Your brother is all over that."

"Gage?"

"Yeah, they got together while you were gone. He didn't tell you?"

"No."

"You thought . . . me and Amber?"

"Yes. You were hanging out with her. And on the couch the other day, you scooted closer to her to make room for me."

He looked up, thinking back. "Oh. That's because you looked super annoyed with her. I thought I was saving you from having to sit by her."

I let out a single laugh. "Stop reading me."

He curled his lip. "Amber? Come on, Charlie, give me some credit." He gripped a section of my T-shirt at my waist. "She wears sparkly words across her butt. You told me not to date anyone who did that." He pressed his lips to mine again. "What about Evan?"

"Yeah, no." I traced the words on his T-shirt with my finger. "It would be hard to be with someone when I couldn't stop thinking about someone else."

"That night by the fence, when you thought I was going to tell you that I liked you . . ."

"You don't need to explain."

He shook his head. "No. I do. I did like you. But I had convinced myself I couldn't tell you that. I didn't want to ruin our friendship. So you caught me off guard because it wasn't what I was going to tell you that night. It freaked me out a little that you knew I liked you anyway. I wasn't sure how you would take it, how your family would take it."

"And now?"

"And now I'm still not sure how your family will take it, but that night, you were so hurt, it made me hopeful that at least you would take it well. I thought maybe you were telling me that night that you liked me too, and for the first time it gave me reason to think that it wouldn't ruin anything."

"I don't know how my brothers will react, but my dad loves you."

He buried his face against my neck. "Gage already knows."

I tried to push him away so I could look at his face. He wouldn't budge. "What did he say?"

"He's mad."

I finally managed to push him away and look at him. The first thing I saw was the black beneath his right eye. "Wait. Did Gage do that to you?"

"What?"

I ran a finger lightly along the black.

"Oh. No."

"So it was a golf ball, then?"

He shook his head no. "It was . . ." His eyes looked around me but not at me. "My dad."

I sat up quickly and my head went light. "Your dad hit you?"

He smiled, which seemed like the opposite reaction to my statement. "Yes. I finally confronted him. He hit me.

My mom kicked him out."

"Braden! Why didn't you tell me? Are you okay?"

"Yes. For years I've wanted her to kick him out. I didn't realize it would take him hitting me for her to finally do it. I should've confronted him a long time ago." His face was still lit with a smile, but I knew him. I saw hurt in his eyes. He didn't want his dad to leave. He wanted his dad to love him enough to want to change.

"I'm sorry." I ran a hand through his hair, and he moved his head to my lap. We stayed like that for a while, his head resting on me, my fingers combing through his hair. "So why is Gage mad at you?"

"You're his sister, Charlie."

"That makes no sense. He didn't get mad at Evan."

"I think he knows you were never into Evan."

"But he thought I was into you?"

"I don't know. He probably thought I'd have more potential to seriously hurt you. But I won't. I promise I won't. . . . I love you."

My heart slammed against my ribs and my breath left me. I lowered my lips to his. "I love you too."

CHAPTER 36

• • • • • • •

"I will still kill you in football," I said, looking down where he lay in my lap as if he never wanted to move.

"What? I don't get boyfriend perks?"

Hearing him say the word *boyfriend* made my heart burst with joy. Then I immediately felt guilty for being this happy when I'd just found out about my mom. I stared at the cloudless sky.

"Is this too weird? Too fast?"

I took his hand in mine. "No." He was my happiness right now. I wasn't going to give it up.

He reached up and traced a line between my brows,

and I wondered if I was scowling.

"I just feel guilty."

"Because of your mom?"

I nodded. "I feel like I should be in mourning or something."

"Charlie, you've been in mourning for ten years."

"True." The sunlight touched the tips of his dark hair, and his hazel eyes looked brown today.

He gave me a lazy smile. "What?"

"We kissed."

He laughed and sat up, moving behind me. He wrapped me up from behind, pulling me back against his chest. "Am I a better kisser than Evan?"

"Hmmm . . ."

He let out an indignant grunt.

"Is this a competition?"

"Absolutely."

This time I laughed and twisted around, pressing my lips to his. "Yes, Braden, you win." He was an amazing kisser.

The day had turned to dusk when we walked back to my house, kicking the soccer ball back and forth between us as we went.

"So . . ."

He quirked an eyebrow at me. "What?"

"Are you going to tell my family about us, or am I?"

"Probably better if you do. I already have one black eye."

"Funny . . . wait, you don't think my brothers would hit you, do you?"

"I hope not."

Now I was scared. Braden was right; this was different than just some random guy I met. This was Braden. He was practically part of the family. I knew how much pressure that put on us. I knew my brothers and father would understand that as well.

Braden studied my face. "Oh, great. You're terrified. If you're scared, how am I supposed to feel?"

"I already told you to stop reading me."

"I can read you because I know you better."

"In your dreams."

"Yes, you've been there, too."

I backhanded him across the stomach, but couldn't help but smile.

When we walked into the house with a foot of space between us, my dad looked up from the game he was watching—an NBA classic.

"Don't even think about it," I told Braden, whose eyes lit up when he saw what was on television.

"Where have you been, Charlie?" my dad asked. "You're supposed to be grounded."

"Oh, that's right. I forgot."

"You're grounded?" Braden asked. His eyes seemed to say *If you're already grounded, maybe we should tell him later.*

I felt the opposite—if I was already grounded, might as well get this out too. I couldn't get in any more trouble.

"Can we talk?" I asked.

My father's eyes darted to Braden as if searching for clues to what I was about to say. He wasn't going to find his answers from Braden this time.

"Maybe we should get everyone in here," I said.

"Everyone?" Braden asked. "Right now? Don't you just want to talk to your dad first?"

"No. Might as well talk to them all at once."

"This sounds serious," my dad said, finally using the remote to turn off the game.

"It is serious. But good serious."

He narrowed his eyes. "Okay."

I yelled up the stairs to my brothers and soon the three of them, plus my dad, were crammed on our long couch. They barely fit shoulder to shoulder. I stood in front of them with Braden behind me.

I cracked my knuckles and took a deep breath. "Okay. So . . ." I had no idea where to begin. I felt like it needed a lead-in, but what could I tell them that they didn't already know?

Wait. Gage already knew how Braden felt. Had he

told the others? I eyed Gage, and he gave me a rare hard look, daring me to confess to the whole family what he already knew.

My mouth went dry and I tried to swallow. My tongue felt twice as big as it should. Finally, I squeezed my eyes shut and spit out, "I love him." I pointed over my shoulder and opened my eyes at the same time.

Gage's jaw tightened. So he still hadn't gotten used to the idea. Everyone else just stared at me like they were waiting for me to finish my point. They all loved Braden. They didn't understand what I meant.

I reached behind me blindly, hoping he'd help me out. It didn't take him more than a second to put his hand in mine. "We're together," I said.

I wasn't sure who started the outburst, but soon they were all talking at once and it wasn't to congratulate us. Jerom was the first on his feet, and he said, "How dare you take advantage of her right now?" His cold stare was on Braden. They all seemed to stand up in unison after that.

I held up my hand before someone else said something hurtful. "Stop. He is the only one who had the guts to even hint that something more happened with Mom. So don't you dare act like he is taking advantage of me."

Jerom fisted his hands. "It sure seems that way."

"I'm not breakable. Don't you all get that? I can handle

things. I can make my own decisions. This didn't happen today. I've liked him for a while. We just admitted it today."

"I love her, guys," Braden said.

Nathan stepped forward like he was going to give Braden's black eye a match. My dad grabbed him by the arm. "That's enough, boys," he said, and everyone went quiet. "I've asked this young man to keep an eye on Charlie on numerous occasions. How is it fair to now say I don't trust him?"

I could feel the tension drain from Braden next to me.

My father looked at Braden and in a chilling voice said, "You better not betray my trust."

"No, sir."

"Then it's settled. But you're still grounded until the party, Charlie." He looked at Braden. "So get out of here."

Braden had never been kicked out when I was grounded before. But he'd never been mine before, either. I squeezed his hand and he left. As soon as the door shut, my brothers' smiles were back.

"I wondered when he'd say something."

"It was so obvious."

"But, Charlie," Gage said, "I had no idea you felt the same."

I nodded, and they continued to talk about who knew what and when. Then one by one they all went quiet. It was the first time we'd all been in the same place at the same time since I found out about my mom. I had been avoiding this.

I looked at my dad. "I think it's time we all talked about Mom. Together." I grabbed the box full of pictures from beneath the table. I was still beyond angry with her, but I knew the first step to getting through that was to learn more about her from the people who knew her better than I did.

I sat on the couch and opened the box. They all still stood there, staring, like I had asked them who wrote *Pride and Prejudice*. Then Gage snatched a picture from the box and held it up. "This was the day that Nathan pushed me into a tree because he said I was cheating at hide-and-seek. Mom totally took my side, by the way."

"You *were* cheating. You always cheat," Nathan said, sitting next to me and reaching in for a stack of pictures. My brothers all had their hands in the box now and were talking over one another again. I looked up and saw my dad standing there, staring at the pile of pictures on the table. She was in most of them. His expression was hard and it seemed he too was still angry with my mom. But then he met my eyes and his whole aura lightened with a smile. It seemed to say *She gave me you, Charlie, and I'll always love her for that.* That was a lot for an aura to say, but I was sure Linda would've agreed.

CHAPTER 37

• • • • • • •

I held my breath and walked into Bazaar. I'd waited too long to come in, but I was here now. Linda looked up from where she stood behind the register.

"I'm sorry." I didn't know what else to say. There was no good excuse for my lie. I took a few steps closer when she didn't respond. "I think my aura is blue today."

That got a small smile out of her. "I don't understand, Charlie."

"I don't either. I guess I just didn't want you feeling sorry for me. It's been so long since I'd met someone who didn't already know my mother was gone."

I didn't feel like Linda needed to know the specifics of my mom's death. That was something between my family and me. But she didn't deserve the lie I'd told her. Nobody did.

"Are people not allowed to feel sorry for your loss?"

I shrugged. "I'm not good with feelings, apparently."

She approached me and I tensed up, waiting for her lecture or for her to tell me to leave or . . . something. She looked me up and down. "You can't work dressed like that."

"I . . ." I glanced down at my basketball shorts. "I can still work here?"

She placed her hands on my arms in a soft touch, then met my eyes. "Charlie, I'm so sorry for your loss."

My eyes went hot. "Me too."

"If you ever need to talk, I'm here."

"Thank you."

"I got these new silky tops in the last shipment that would look fabulous on you. Do you want to add to your work wardrobe since you didn't bring any clothes?"

I nodded. "I need some jeans, too . . . or a skirt."

Her head snapped up to look at me and I laughed. I hadn't planned on working today, but I didn't want to quit. She retrieved the shirt and a pair of jeans and took them to the register. I followed her. Amber's display of makeup stood in a tall hutch next to me. On a whim, I grabbed some shiny lip gloss and plopped it on the counter.

Linda raised her eyebrows at me but didn't say a word as she rang it up with my clothes.

I paid and tucked the clothes against my chest. "We're having a barbeque at my house tomorrow evening. We do it every year before school starts."

"I don't have you on the schedule for tomorrow."

"No. I was inviting you. Will you come?"

She smiled then. "Yes. I'd love to come."

"Good." I headed to the back to change.

Toward the end of my shift Skye poked her head in from the back room. "Charlie! Come to the beach when you get off. Impromptu bonfire concert."

"Can't. I'm grounded."

She laughed. "Bummer. Next time, then."

"Yes. I'm having a party at my house tomorrow. Will you come?"

"Absolutely." She disappeared into the back. I smiled. It was amazing what happened when you let yourself be open to new things.

I loved our end-of-summer parties. Everyone was back in town from vacation, and people were excited to have one last event. They came in packs. There were at least fifty people in my backyard. Even more this year. I shut my curtains and turned back to face Amber.

She had talked me into letting her do my makeup for the event. She pointed out that I didn't have to wear this much all the time, but it was always nice for special occasions. I let her, because she was right. It was nice to step out of my comfort zone every once in a while.

"You look great," she said as I pulled my hair up in an elastic band.

I smiled. "Thanks."

She giggled to herself then said, "You hated me at that baseball game, didn't you?"

"What? No."

"I was there with Braden, fawning all over him, talking about how cute he was."

"Okay, maybe a little."

She laughed. "Well, I never stood a chance. Did I ever tell you about how when you went away to basketball camp he talked about you nonstop?" She deepened her voice and then said, "'Charlie loves golf. If Charlie were here she'd order meat lover's pizza. Charlie hates romantic comedies.'" She smiled. "It all worked out in the end, though, because Gage is a better match for me anyway."

I laughed. "Come on, let's go down."

"Okay."

We stepped into the backyard. My dad and Jerom manned the barbeque. Nathan and Gage threw a football back and forth in the far corner of the yard. People swam and ate and talked. I was so happy.

A pair of arms wrapped around me from behind. "Football later?"

I leaned back into Braden. "Yes."

"I've missed you this week."

"Me too."

He kissed my cheek. "I'm going to get some food. I'll be right back." He took off across the yard to join my dad and Jerom at the barbeque.

Dave walked across the grass, holding his soda. I nodded to Amber. "I'm going to go mingle."

"Okay."

"You should join Gage. Catch a few footballs."

"Yeah, right."

I pointed to my face and the makeup there.

She laughed. "Fine. I'll try."

"Exactly."

I walked over to face Dave, a long-overdue apology forming on my lips, and the first thing he said was, "I was never scared of your brothers."

"Um . . . what?"

"That's not why I didn't ask you out. I was scared of Braden."

I laughed. "Fair enough." I toed the grass with my foot, having a hard time coming up with the right words.

"I'm sorry about your grandma, Dave." He might not have known how I felt at the time, but I knew I needed to apologize. I had been insensitive.

He smiled. "Thanks, Charlie. That really means a lot."

I nodded, then whirled around and almost pushed Braden's plate full of food into his chest.

"Whoa," he said, lifting it in the air and saving it.

"Sorry."

He nodded at Dave, who said, "Hey, Braden. Thanks again, Charlie."

"Of course."

Dave left, heading for the pool.

Braden gave me a smirk. "That was nice."

"I'm nice sometimes."

He held out the plate. "I got food for you."

"Aw. You do know the way to my heart."

We sat at a table and ate off the same plate.

"Uh oh," Braden said when I snatched the last chip.

"Did you want it?"

"No. It's just . . . your brothers are headed this way and they have a mischievous look in their eyes."

I turned around and had less than three seconds to process before Gage grabbed hold of one of my arms. I knew what was happening even before Nathan took the other one.

"Don't! You'll ruin my makeup."

Jerom grabbed my feet with a laugh. "Has she ever said that before in her life?" They picked me up and carried me toward the pool.

"Seriously. You are all going in if you do this."

"Braden? Aren't you going to help us?" Gage asked.

He held up his hands. "And face her wrath? I think I'm out."

"Aren't you going to help *me*?" I asked.

His eyes twinkled. "No."

"Dead. You're all dead to me."

"I just wanted to see if I learned how to throw someone into a body of water," Jerom said. "I was taught how last month and I need to test it out."

I got my foot loose and kicked him in the chest.

He grabbed his chest muscle. "Ouch. That hurts worse than it looks."

"Right?" Gage said. "Why do you think I got her arm this time?"

"I hate all of you."

"You love us." They reached the edge of the pool and threw me in with a big arching swing.

I surfaced, spitting water. "You better get Amber next."

I heard a shriek and I laughed. Braden did a cannonball next to me, fully clothed. I dunked him back under when he came up.

The second time he came up with his half smile, I pulled him into a hug. "You knew you'd end up in here anyway, so you thought you'd join me on your own, huh?"

"No. You wouldn't have gotten me. I was just hot."

"Whatever, I totally would've gotten you."

He shrugged, his eyes green with the water reflecting in them. "I guess we'll never know."

"Which means I win," we both said at the same time.

He kissed me. "Then how come I feel like the winner?"

It was still dark when my eyes fluttered open. I stared at the ceiling for a while, unsure of what woke me. It wasn't a nightmare. My phone chimed on my desk. I swung my feet to the ground and stood. I didn't pick it up to read the message. I just smiled and ran outside to the fence. The moon was full tonight, perfect for a chat.

ACKNOWLEDGMENTS

• • • • • • •

I'd like to start off by thanking my amazing readers. You are all the best encouragers any author could ask for. Whenever I'm feeling insecure (which is more often than not), I can always count on you to brighten my day and give me the motivation to keep writing. So thank you!

As always, this book wouldn't exist without some very amazing people: Agent Extraordinaire Michelle Wolfson, Editor Supreme Sarah Landis, the ever-awesome Alice Jerman, and the rest of the HarperTeen team. Thank you for all your wisdom, insight, and support.

Even before making it to the in-box of my editor or agent, I have some brilliant beta readers that help whip it into shape: Stephanie Ryan, Candice Kennington, Jenn Johansson, Renee Collins, Natalie Whipple, Michelle Davidson Argyle, Sara Raasch, Julie Nelson, and Kari Olson. I love these ladies. They are my very closest friends.

I'd also like to thank some other authors who helped guide me through my debut year: Ellen Oh, Elsie Chapman, Megan Shepherd, Erin Bowman, Brandy Colbert, Shannon Messenger, Alexandra Duncan, April Tucholke, and Mindy McGinnis. Thanks for sharing the journey with me.

And, of course, I wouldn't be able to write at all if not for the support of my best friend and husband, Jared, and my amazing kids, Hannah, Autumn, Abby, and Donavan. I truly feel so blessed to be their mom. Speaking of moms, mine is amazing. Thanks, Mom, for everything.

Since this is a book about brothers, I feel the need to personally thank mine for teaching me how awesome (and pesky) brothers can be. I couldn't have written this book without knowing the bond a girl can share with her brothers. Love you, Jared and Spencer.

I have the world's best, most supportive (and very large) family. If I attempt to name them all, I'm sure I will leave someone out and then I will feel guilty for life. So I will just say thanks to my parents-in-law: Vance and Karen (whom I adore); to all my sisters: Heather, Stephanie, Rachel D, Zita, Shar, Rachel B, Angie, and Emily; to the rest of my brothers: Eric, Brian, Jim, Rick, Dave, and Kevin; and to all the kids who go with all these people. I love you all.

MORE FROM KASIE WEST

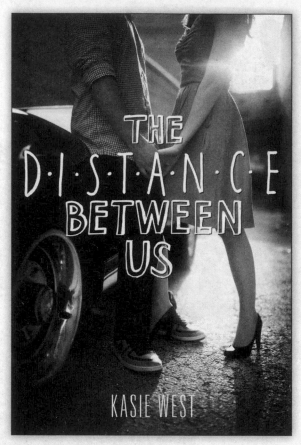

Seventeen-year-old Caymen Meyers learned early that the rich are not to be trusted. Enter Xander Spence—he's tall, handsome, and oozing rich. But just when Xander's attention and loyalty are about to convince Caymen that being rich isn't a character flaw, she finds out that money is a much bigger part of their relationship than she'd ever realized.

With so many obstacles standing in their way, can she close the distance between them?